Uncivil Liberties

Uncivil Liberties

*Congress shall make no law respecting an establishment
of religion, or prohibiting the free exercise thereof;
or abridging the freedom of speech . . . .*

Religion and speech clauses of the
First Amendment to the United States Constitution

Bernie Lambek

Rootstock Publishing

First Printing: May 25, 2018

ISBN-10: 1-57869-006-4
ISBN-13: 978-1-57869-006-0
Library of Congress Control Number: 2017.963.963

Published by Rootstock Publishing
an imprint of Multicultural Media, Inc.
www.rootstockpublishing.com
info@rootstockpublishing.com

This is a work of fiction. A few real people are mentioned in passing,
though I gave some of them fictional stories. One real person is featured
at length, Judge Guido Calabresi of the Second Circuit Court of Appeals;
the dialogue I have attributed to him is entirely made-up. The remainder
of the characters are fictional though some may bear non-coincidental
resemblances to real people. Montpelier, Vermont, is real. Its streets, parks
and merchants have fictional names, but many Vermonters will recognize
the places.

Email the author at blambek@zclpc.com

Cover art by Susan Bull Riley
Author photo by Ken Russell
Cover and book design by D. Hoffman

Printed in the USA

Dedication

*To my late parents, Hanna Weiss Lambek
and Joachim Lambek*

Contents

Part I
A Death in Montpelier

She woke up thinking about her. Went to sleep thinking about her. Eating, bathing, French class, jogging, always thinking about her. In the hallway between classes, she caught a glimpse of her and their eyes locked and she felt a jolt of inspiration in her veins. She could become a woman this way. I can do this, she thought. In practice their sleeves brushed and she could smell perfumed skin, and when her head turned to her to whisper an encouragement she could smell her breath and the girl became intoxicated. No, I can't do this, it is impossible, she also thought. I am fucking crazy.

On a hill to the north of Montpelier sits Mahady Park, a thousand acres of tall pines and mixed deciduous woods. Sheer granite outcrops overlook the town. Trails meander through the park. A couple of open shelters, one near the park entrance off Smiley Street, the other higher up, near the fire tower, are used for picnics and barbecues, even in winter. Ah, Vermonters.

Snow had fallen a few days earlier and lay in scattered patches over the dark ground on this cold morning in November. Before dawn, a man walking his dog along the trail that skirts the bottom of one of the steep outcrops came upon a body. He didn't notice her at first, in the dim light below the ledge.

He was picking his way carefully along the trail, stepping over roots and rocks, a mournful fiddle tune running through his head, his old dog snuffling along beside him. He smelled the familiar dampness of the woods and the earth. The dog stopped to inspect a lumpy shape at the side of the trail, among the rocks and maple leaf detritus. Water dripped down the granite ledge, audible in the stillness. The man stepped closer, and he then saw the shape was a girl, twisted awkwardly in her down jacket, her eyes open and clouded. A denim cloth handbag was near the body.

He spun around. No one else was there. He muttered an oath to the dog, and they hurried home. In fifteen minutes he was on the phone with the Montpelier police.

Soon the cops were at the spot below the cliff. They found identification in a pocket of the handbag, but Sergeant LaPorte already knew who the girl was. They all knew her mother, Deputy State's Attorney Francine Loughlin. Barry LaPorte held his breath as he looked down at young Kerry Pearson, innocent and dead. All he said was "Shit" and then he looked up at the wet granite cliff. Thirty feet, he guessed. There was a trail near the top, not so close to the edge. This had never happened before; no one had ever fallen over the ledge. And no one had jumped.

Sam Jacobson woke up because Donna was downstairs in the kitchen banging last night's pots and dishes as she put them away. He would have kept sleeping had the house been still. Wispy remnants of his last dream—he's in the courtroom, a client brazenly accusing him of malpractice, Judge Affonco grinning in agreement, banging his gavel—evaporated as the gavel became the pots downstairs and he felt his foot tangled in the twisted sheet, and his mind slowly located the real world.

He yanked up the shade and looked outside. What he saw matched his mood, grey and damp and depressed. The sugar maple on the front lawn had lost its rusty salmon leaves and now stood bare. The neighbor across the street with the howling Airedale was scraping frost off the Subaru windshield. Looking west, he could see the church steeples and the tower of Montpelier City Hall, built to mimic an Italian fortress, poking up above the downtown buildings.

He did his bathroom routine, got dressed, kissed Donna, his wife, who kissed him back. He read parts of the paper, ate his yogurt, and headed on foot to his regular coffeehouse a few doors from his law office on Chamber Street.

Montpelier—pronounced by Vermonters and *cognoscenti* more or less as MuntPEELier, with the accent on the middle syllable, unlike its French cousin—is the hub of a rural landscape of quiet rolling pastures, woodlots and a few remaining small dairy farms, flanked on the northwest by the dark mass of the Abenaki Mountain Range. The farmland, grim and spare this time of year, is dotted with villages and working granite quarries and also scarred by a strip of car showrooms and service centers, and an ugly shopping mall up on the hill by the hospital—the same hospital where Sam's daughter Sarah was born and Donna's knee was rebuilt, on separate occasions.

On this blustery weekday morning in Montpelier, commuters from the surrounding villages and back roads drove with care, peering through the patch of windshield cleared by the defroster. A few pedestrians navigated sidewalks slick with frost. Steam coated the windows of the Sacred Grounds Café. Inside the café, a rustic orange tile countertop graced the street-side window, two worn sofas backed up against the far wall next to a table with insulated coffee urns and paraphernalia, and eight or ten wooden tables with unmatched chairs and assorted stools haphazardly straddled the space in front of the kitchen and service counter.

A line of customers already stretched back from the counter. Next to the queue stood shelves crowded with pound bags of coffee beans, whole or ground, French presses, Italian percolators, and mugs for sale. Some customers left with their hot coffee and scones; others found a table or a stool by the window, greeted friends, read *The Central Vermont Argus*, worked on a laptop, or did nothing but stare at the steamy window.

Had it been clear, they would have seen the county courthouse, across the street and up a half-block, red brick with white columns in front and a handsome clock tower above, with the simple symmetry of a New England church. Directly across Chamber Street sat a Dunkin Donuts, almost empty.

Sam pulled off his beret, leaving his salt-and-pepper hair disheveled. His face had grown heavy in the past few years, with extra padding around the eyes, like he'd been in the boxing ring one too many times. He had lost some of the dark intensity that had marked his youthful face, which had so attracted the young college student named Donna Lowbeer in New Haven many years before. His mid-section was a bit heavy too, now, and his gait was slow and deliberate.

He breathed in the aroma of dark roasted coffee and fresh cornmeal muffins, and saw Ricky Stillwell at the tile counter facing the window. Sam hadn't seen his young friend for some time, and usually enjoyed hearing what was on Ricky's mind. "Hey Ricky," he called out. Ricky looked up quickly from his laptop with an awkward fleeting smile.

The boy was tall and angular and wary. He was a senior at Montpelier High, very smart, Sam thought, but also odd and standoffish. Ricky's mom, Clara, was a case worker for state human services and she sat on the Montpelier school board. His dad, Carver, was a woodworker who made fine furniture and was almost mute by disposition. Sam and Donna bought an oak table from him years earlier.

The couples had been friendly since Ricky's older sister Meg and their own daughter Sarah were in fifth grade together and played soccer. The parents had huddled on the sidelines, cheering, cold, and commiserating. The girls were now out of college, out in the world.

For Sam, though, the friendship with the Stillwells, going on fifteen years now, had always been stressed by discord over religion.

People in Montpelier mostly avoided the subject of religious belief. Those who went to church sang hymns and listened to homilies, and when that was done, they preferred to talk about community projects. Or the place of religion in history, such as the recent book discussion at the synagogue about Jews in the Middle Ages. Others swore that last week's film at the Bijou, a grim documentary about receding glaciers, was spiritual.

But they did not talk frankly and openly about the content of their beliefs. What do you believe about God? Does God intervene in human affairs? Does the soul exist outside the body? These were questions best avoided, as if they would invade a person's privacy, like asking when you last masturbated.

Ricky's mom, Clara Stillwell, was different. From the start, Clara, a devout believer in the divinity of Christ, corralled Sam Jacobson during occasional picnics or dinners at the Jacobson house, or even as they congregated at the perimeter of the soccer fields, standing elbow to elbow or seated under blankets in their fold-up chairs, where she examined him like a hostile witness. She thought Sam exhibited an unholy and incongruous mix of Judaism and atheism. Sam agreed his beliefs were unholy. But incongruous?

On more than one occasion, provoked by the righteous Clara Stillwell, Sam had made an effort to explain he was a Jew because of history, not faith, and an atheist because of reason, again not faith. "Look," he said, sounding pompous even to his own ears, "I just don't believe in the truth of the scriptures or a supreme being or the eternal soul, or karma for that matter. Not literally, anyway."

Metaphorically, fine; he could abide metaphors, as long as they were marinated in humor, but a sense of humor did not feature prominently in Clara's repertoire. As he put it to Clara in his lawyerly way, he would follow the evidence and believe what the evidence revealed.

"Oh, I have evidence," she said one time while they waited for breakfast to be served at the venerable Byway Diner out on Route 302, where they liked to take the kids on Saturday mornings after early soccer practice. The girls and Ricky—he was about five at the time—occupied their own booth, out of hearing distance. Donna and Carver sat mute, tolerating their spouses.

"No," he argued, tugging in frustration on the beard he wore in those years, "one person's anecdote is not good evidence."

"Millions of people," she retorted.

"What you have is millions of people who *believe*," Sam instructed. "But belief doesn't bootstrap itself into knowledge. People believe all kinds of things. I mean, millions of people believe in astrology." Bad example; maybe she believed in astrology. "And angels." Maybe she believed in angels too. He thought of a better example. "Millions believe in Santa Claus, for Christ's sake."

Clara peered at him, her brown frizzy hair pulled back and held tight by a clasp in the shape of a fish. "Now you want to compare God to Santa Claus?" She had an intimidating way of leaning forward from her hips, her spine rigid. The waitress brought their omelets and poured more coffee.

"Oh, jeez," he said with typical irritation, and then realized she was right. "Okay, yes, Clara, in a way. God is a character who appears in literature around the world for the last three millennia. Or perhaps lots of characters. At least there are lots of versions of him. He's complex and interesting," he would give her that, "but a fictional character nonetheless. And a cruel one, by the way," he added. "If you remember Job. These are stories."

Clara bristled. "First God is Santa Claus, now he's"—she searched for the right reference—"Captain Ahab. Or maybe Sherlock Holmes. There're lots of fictional versions of Sherlock Holmes. I saw one on TV who's nothing like the original Sherlock Holmes from the BBC. So you think God is a made-up sea captain with OCD, or he's an arrogant English detective with a cocaine addiction. That's your position, Attorney Jacobson?"

Donna, eating toast, tilted her head at Carver and smiled with her blue-grey eyes. Carver raised one eyebrow in silent acknowledgment of their comradeship.

"Elementary, my dear Clara," said Sam, who wished sorely to defuse the argument but did just the opposite. "Well no," he then clarified, "God is definitely not Sherlock Holmes, who is the paragon of rationality, nothing like God."

"You have too much faith in rationality," she said with a note of triumph.

"You have too much faith in faith," he said. And just so he could end on a winning strike, he added, "And by the way, Clara, the original Sherlock Holmes was not the one from the BBC."

He signaled the waitress for the check. "For that table too," he told the waitress, nodding to the kids' booth. "I'll cover it this time," he said to Clara and Carver.

His Jewishness was something else again; he had inherited a history, a story of a people, a race. "I don't choose to be Jewish," he told Clara another time. "It was dished out to me."

Not like Christians, he didn't add, who are the masters of conversion and possess an uncanny aptitude for being born again.

And so it went over the years, the conversation recurring in various guises. Clara was neither persuaded nor appeased. She wanted certainty. She despised moral relativism, an intellectual defect she falsely attributed to Sam. "On what foundation," Clara asked, "can we find a morality to guide us, if not revealed in scripture, the Word of God?" And yet, Sam noticed, at other times Clara talked as if everything were determined by fate, by the unfolding of the heavenly plan. But then, if that were the case, what room was left for a person to choose to act morally? That was where the incongruity lay, Sam tried to explain to Clara. Fate or free will, but not both.

The gulf between their worldviews might have kept them apart, yet each was attracted to the challenge the other posed. And their relationship was not, of course, limited to arguments about God and history. One winter night early in their acquaintance, an accident brought them together after a Montpelier school board meeting. The hour was late and several inches of fresh snow were on the roads when they left the meeting. Clara hit a bad patch of snow and her little Honda skidded off the road a half mile from the school where Route 2 turns sharply to the bridge across the Scape River, the Honda hovering at the edge of the steep bank down to the river.

Sam came upon Clara's car a moment later and pulled up and stopped behind her. He scrambled over to the side of the Honda and saw that Clara was petrified. He helped her out of the car and wrapped her in a blanket he retrieved from the back of his minivan. He called the Bob's Sunoco hotline from his cell, and they waited together in his minivan with the heater running. Clara sat shivering in her blanket and Sam leaned across and reached his arm around her, awkward at first, and held her and warmed her. They sat like this for 20 minutes before help in the form of a tow-truck arrived. They did not talk about religion or much of anything else. After this event, Clara occasionally introduced Sam to her friends as her Jewish savior.

After a soccer match three or four years later when the girls were seniors in high school—it was the game Meg Stillwell had scored the winning goal against Middlefield—the two families met at DaVinci's to celebrate over wood-fired pizza and the topic of religious belief arose once again, as if wafted into the air with the scent of roasted garlic.

Ricky, ten years old by that time, chewing pepperoni, faced the adults. "Religions are all different," he said, as if challenging them to a duel. "Like whether Jesus is the son of God or not. Or is heaven real. We learned about Mohammed in school, like he was a prophet. But none of you think he is. And there's Hindus and Buddhists—they're totally different. How do you know who's right? They can't all be right." A dribble of grease rolled down the heel of his hand and he grabbed a napkin and wiped himself clean.

"You mean they're incompatible?" Sam asked, eyebrows raised.

"Yeah, incompatible," said Ricky, drawing his mother's glower.

For Sam, that was as good an argument as most in favor of atheism. But Ricky soon spun in the opposite direction. They can't all be right, so at the fragile age of thirteen, he chose one, decisively, and became a devotee of the Fellowship Church of the Crucified Savior, which billed itself as a nondenominational born-again faith community. The church was newly built in a field beyond the Montpelier High School.

Ricky's headstrong choice troubled his Baptist mother, who was nervous about her son's rambling independence. On the other hand, the development led, perversely, to an intellectual bond with lawyer Sam Jacobson. Ricky began to stop at Sam's office after school and learned how to read and understand Supreme Court opinions. He debated with Sam, and the lawyer found his day enlivened by the challenge. From their opposite poles they met at the crossroads of the First Amendment. So when Sam sued the Town of Jefferson on behalf of one Lucy Cross, who objected to the prayer delivered at the start of town meeting, Ricky's interest was sparked. He skipped school to attend the oral argument in federal court in Burlington. He and Sam became allies.

When town officials, Sam had argued, invite the local Christian minister, year after year, to deliver a prayer at the annual town meeting—where the citizens gather to deliberate and vote on public business, like the purchase of a new grader or installation of a new culvert—the town inevitably promotes Christianity, *establishing* a religion in violation of the First Amendment. He didn't persuade the judge.

He did persuade Ricky. For Ricky, the government's sponsorship of religion by means of the annual prayer cheapened and defiled Christianity. He wanted to keep the government's profane hands off religion to preserve its sanctity. Sam (and the brave, despised Lucy Cross) wanted to keep the government out of religious practice, and vice versa, for different reasons: to preserve a secular democracy of equal citizens and to protect minorities, atheists among them, from being marginalized.

The judge, in the end, ruled that history and tradition provided an adequate nonreligious justification. The practice of prayer at town meeting is an acknowledgment of religion, she ruled, not an establishment of religion. This was a nice distinction that neither Sam nor Ricky could figure out. The case was now on appeal before the Second Circuit Court of Appeals in New York. Ricky told Sam he would attend that argument too. He had become a First Amendment *aficionado*.

But now at the Sacred Grounds Café, just weeks after Sam had filed Lucy Cross's appeal, Ricky Stillwell was distant and aloof. "Hey Sam," he replied in kind, but turned away, working his jaw with clenched teeth, and closed his laptop. "Gotta go to school, class is about to start."

Sam watched him leave without another word. Through a clearing in the window, he could see Ricky head down the street with his long rolling stride. He joined the line at the counter, clutching the insulated mug he had brought in his briefcase. He had purchased the mug from the Sacred Grounds; it bore the logo *Coffee is my creed*. Even at his age, Sam's feelings were hurt by Ricky's behavior in a way he couldn't define.

In the gloom below the cliff, Sergeant LaPorte crouched gingerly next to Kerry Pearson's body. A fellow officer had climbed to the top of the outcrop, and was peering over the top. "Nothing of interest up here," he called down.

LaPorte's knees and back grew sore as he squatted next to Kerry's contorted body, and he maneuvered into a kneeling position on the wet leaves, as if in prayer. The wet quickly soaked through his pants, and he felt the discomfort and continued to look at the girl. Her face was turned up in a frozen expression of anticipation.

She had been a pretty girl. Her blond hair was tangled and splayed amid the leaves. She wore black stretch pants, a blue, down-filled jacket, unzipped, and beneath it a sweatshirt with writing. He lifted one side of the jacket and revealed a quotation from Margaret Mead: *Never doubt that a small group of thoughtful, committed citizens can change the world.* Her mother, he thought, the good prosecutor: she was a committed citizen changing the world. And perhaps this girl, Kerry Pearson, was too. Or she would have been, had she lived.

He noticed blood matted into her hair at the back. There was blood too on a strip of rock ledge next to her. He did not want to lift her head. He sighed heavily as he looked at her dead eyes. A third officer began to snap photos, the flash startling and intrusive, bathing Kerry Pearson in white light.

He notified dispatch and called the state medical examiner and then called Francine Loughlin at home, saying only that he needed to meet with her right away, and could they meet at her house? LaPorte had occasion before to tell a parent her child was dead. But this was different.

He knew Frannie. They had worked cases together for years, including the most depraved child sex abuse crimes. He was a big tough man with scars, and a sensitive core that always surprised his colleagues.

He wouldn't admit it now, but he wanted to be the one to tell Francine about her daughter's death. He had children too and he believed he understood the deep pool of loss this meant. More than that: he had an unspoken sentimental attachment to this prosecutor, which had begun even years before his marriage ended. He ached for her now, in a way that embarrassed him.

There was another reason this was different. This was a suicide.

The cops found a note in Kerry's handbag. The denim cloth bag contained just a few items. There was her wallet, a cell phone, a tube of hand lotion, a toothbrush in a plastic sleeve, a small tube of toothpaste, a date book, three keys on a ring, a pair of tan leather gloves, lip gloss, a book called *Animal, Vegetable, Miracle*, a bunch of tissues, and a scrap of a suicide note, written on a torn piece of paper.

Several minutes later, Sergeant LaPorte climbed onto the porch of the small yellow house on Baker Street with neighbors tight on each side. The house glowed with a fresh coat of paint and was surrounded by a well-tended lawn and flower garden. He met Francine at her door.

Her eyes were swollen and red. She looked him over. "Your knees are all wet, Barry." Her big friend with wet knees, and she now noticed, wet eyes, stood on her porch. "What's going on?" she said.

"Fran, can I come in? Let's sit down." They went in. They sat at the kitchen table facing each other. She wore a night dress covered with a loose cream robe. Her hair was the color of pumpkin and it fell across her shoulders.

"Tell me," she said. "It's Kerry, right? She didn't come home last night. She's done that before, slept over with friends after a late night. She's 17." She stopped. "Barry, tell me, whatever it is."

He reached across the table and put his hand over hers. "Yes, it's Kerry."

Outside, the sky was changing from the color of slate to an oyster shell. There was no soft way. "Fran, Kerry died last night. Her . . ."

"No!"

". . . body was found this morning in Mahady Park."

"No!"

"At the bottom of a cliff there."

He placed his other hand around hers and imagined he gave her strength with his own vital force, from his skin, warming and penetrating hers. "I am so, so sorry, Frannie."

She stared at him. His words seemed completely useless at this moment. His knees were cold and damp. He felt a tremor in her hands.

"Fran, it looks like she took her own life."

"What!"

"She left a note in her handbag."

Fran made another small exclamation and then stilled, as Barry's words entered her and played for recognition against all of her instincts. She yanked her hands back and turned to the window, folding inward on herself, like she had turned off the power switch.

She sat there for some seconds, breathing, her eyes open but vacant, so that Barry even wondered if she had lost consciousness. Through the window he watched two squirrels frantically chasing each other around the single butternut tree in the side yard.

"Killed herself?" she then muttered. "That can't be, she would never do that."

In a minute she looked back at Barry and asked, "How can you be sure? How do you know?"

"The note seems clear, Frannie. I'm so sorry. May I show you the note now? You'll know her handwriting. You can tell us for sure."

Barry placed a clear ziplock bag on the table between them. Fran looked for several seconds at the paper inside the bag. There it was, just two lines in Kerry's cursive script:

> *I can't go on anymore.*
> *I'm sorry.*

Francine's hands were on the table. Her body folded forward, her face torn by pain. Barry stayed still in his seat across from her and waited.

She eventually said, "Kerry was really upset, stewing over things at school. There was shit going on. I didn't know what it was." Then she made a guttural cry and jacked upright. "I have to call her dad. I want to see her now. Oh God! What do I do? Can you call the school to say she won't be in school today? Call Gayle Peters, she's the principal."

She stood up, teetering. "Do I need a coat, Barry? Tell me what to do."

He asked her if she would like to get dressed first, and she was astonished to find she was not yet dressed. He sent her up to her bedroom with instructions and when she was ready he brought her out to his car. He took his cell phone out to make a call.

LaPorte drove Francine to the Gibson Falls barracks, which doubled as the medical examiner's offices. The ambulance was waiting for them when they arrived, with the body of Kerry Pearson laid out in the back. Francine did what they asked her to do, but she could not pull away for several minutes and she stood rooted to her spot staring at her daughter's body.

After a time LaPorte coaxed her away and took her home, reluctantly leaving her there alone, as she forbade him from calling anyone for support. He decided he would be the one to take care of Francine Loughlin, or at least ask her if she would let him.

At the high school, the call was answered by Barbara Laval, the principal's administrative assistant. It was a phone call from a policeman, asking to speak with Principal Peters. There was nothing alarming in his steady voice.

Barb went out to the entrance lobby to retrieve Gayle Peters where she greeted students. Barb admired the principal's talent, finding something complimentary to say to every student. "Very cute sweater, Siena," Gayle said and smiled at the girl called Siena, as Barb approached.

Gayle's straight dark hair was blessed with a narrow streak of silver, which lent her an air of sophistication. She was just 42, but had been principal at Montpelier High for eight years, as well as the girls' lacrosse coach. She had the trust and admiration of the school board because of her efficiency and ambition, precisely the traits that had cost her the trust and affection of some of the high school's faculty.

But she had loyal friends and supporters too, and students seemed to like her and respect her. It was well known that her lacrosse squad was devoted to her. Barb Laval thought she was a good boss. They were not friends.

Gayle rushed back to her office for the call, anxiety creasing her face, and closed the door. Barb sat in the outer office, with a large glass view to the hallway, watching the kids arriving and milling and fooling around and moving to their lockers and homerooms. They came to school in T-shirts and no coats, so exposed, when it was only in the twenties outside. Barb had grown up in Montreal, a colder place than Vermont, but still she shivered as she watched the bare-armed students.

She herself wore a wool cardigan sweater the color of applesauce which came down to her thighs, and she pulled the big collar around her neck and ears. She turned her thoughts to Alicia, and to the warmth of her kisses that morning.

She and Alicia Santana were married two years before in a ceremony at the Unitarian Church in Montpelier. They'd had eight years of life together, first as an unofficial couple and later in a sanctioned civil union, while Vermont evolved around them in the struggle to adopt same-sex marriage. As couples go, they were happy together, despite Barb's occasional disquiet over how she, dowdy and uncertain, could have earned the love of the fiercely intelligent lawyer, wild and beautiful Alicia Santana.

She was, therefore, smiling to herself when Gayle Peters suddenly opened her office door and bid Barb to come inside, with a quick assessing glance. Gayle at times seemed put off by her assistant's demeanor of dreamy contentment, and by her clothes, Barb suspected, which to Gayle's discerning eye must look frumpy. She would never voice her displeasure, but Barb could sense their separation nonetheless.

The principal said, "There is some terrible news, Barb."

They sat down, and Gayle told her about Kerry Pearson. Barb heard the words and sat looking at Gayle Peters and held up her hand to slow Gayle down so that her mind could catch up to the words and grasp what Gayle was telling her. She looked at Gayle talking to her, and saw, beneath the polished features and the striking white streak in her dark hair, what she suddenly recognized as profound despair. Oh! She impulsively reached forward and brought Gayle into an awkward embrace, surprising them both.

They had never hugged before.

Gayle said, "Thank you. You are such a solid rock for me,"

confounding Barb, who felt nothing like a rock, even at the best of times.

Then there was a rush of events and Barb felt like she was bobbing in a torrent. School superintendent Allen Bird arrived at the school, followed by the grim Sergeant Barry LaPorte. LaPorte, it appeared, was carrying Kerry's suicide note in its ziplock bag.

He wanted, he said, in the course of relating the morning's events, to confirm the note's authenticity. He placed the bag on the round conference table in the principal's office. They leaned in and stared at it.

Barb Laval was dispatched to the classroom of Kerry Pearson's teacher-advisor, John Carruthers, a physics teacher of middle age and unhealthy habits, to procure a sample of Kerry's handwritten school work. Carruthers, with Kerry's latest assignment papers in hand, walked Barb back toward the office, not yet certain what this was all about.

In the hallway, while students filed into their homerooms, the French teacher from Senegal, Dominique Petitbec, waylaid Carruthers to enlighten him on the latest round of negotiations for a new teachers' contract. But Barb intervened. "Dominique, not now, we have got to get back to the principal's office," and she pulled John away from the protesting Madame Petitbec.

"Barb, what the fuck's going on here?" Carruthers demanded. Barb refused to tell, and ushered him through the crowded hallway to Principal Peters's office.

Reconvened around the conference table, they examined the distinctive script on the short note side by side with Kerry's school assignment. No, there was no doubt that Kerry had written the note. Peters enlightened the stunned Carruthers.

Ensconced in her oversized wool cardigan, Barb was struck by a dark memory, a confrontation with her father, who lacked the gene for empathy and whose love for her, tentative and miserly at best, was extinguished as he finally recognized her sexual iniquity. Yet she had never considered suicide. How could Kerry Pearson?

Kerry was the most sensible kid at school, unusually mature and considerate—but, yes, sometimes Kerry was pensive, even sad. Barb had seen this look on Kerry's face at times as Kerry watched her classmates' hallway antics, a look of sad understanding and disappointment that resonated with Barb as she observed Kerry observing her classmates.

Barb then realized she was crying, and the others in the room were silent and patient. Sergeant Barry LaPorte's doleful face softened and he put his strong hand on Barb's, as he had held Francine's hand in his a short time before.

"May we," Gayle Peters asked after a moment, "share this information publicly? People will want to know—will need to know—what happened."

LaPorte cautioned her that the matter was under investigation and no definite conclusions could yet be drawn. "But I understand the need to disclose at least some information," he told her. "Use your discretion, especially about this note here. Please don't, for example, tell folks precisely what is written on the note."

"Yes, yes, of course, we understand that," Peters said, looking for affirmation from Barb and the superintendent and Carruthers. Kerry Pearson's words were sheltered, her compact proclamation of despair preserved from public view.

Peters thanked the officer as he was departing, and asked Barb to gather the high school's administrative and guidance team. They would call a school-wide assembly, she determined, and offer counseling as needed. They would share certain information with the school community. The students needed to know what happened to their classmate, and to hear it here, and to know there was support for them. They would permit Kerry's friends to arrange to leave for the day. Gayle Peters was in charge and could manage a crisis.

And while Gayle was managing the crisis, Barb stole a moment to call Alicia at her Chamber Street law office. Alicia had just arrived and picked up the phone. Barb began to spill out the story and was desperate to hear Alicia's buoyant voice, but then immediately cursed herself as she pictured Alicia reeling from the news. In her dazed mind, Barb had forgotten what she knew perfectly well—Alicia was an old law school friend of Kerry's mother, Francine Loughlin, and had been especially close to Kerry herself when she was little. "I'm a fucking idiot," Barb muttered next to the phone's mouthpiece, and now Alicia was trying to sort it all out.

"What happened? What—what happened? *Barb*!"

Barb tried to explain, but the sequence got confused. Then she was called back to duty and she hung up, cut off, scarcely containing the bile of panic inside her.

In the auditorium at 9:30 a.m., before the entire student body, Principal Gayle Peters stood next to the podium and urged quiet. "We have some sad news, some awful news, to share with you." This drew all their attention and there was a momentary stillness. "It concerns our senior class member, Kerry Pearson."

The principal's voice became soft. Her hand came up to brush the tear on her eyelash, on into her dark hair, where it stayed as she looked into the audience with deep tenderness. "I have to tell you, dear members of our school community, I have to tell you, Kerry Pearson has died."

There were scattered gasps and cries. The principal gathered her resolution, both arms crossed now over her chest. "Oh, this is a terrible loss. I am so sorry. You will hear things around. I don't want there to be rumors and confusion. The police do think that Kerry took her own life. You should understand that. We don't know everything about this." Students were sobbing.

Then a sudden bustle and clatter: Ricky Stillwell pushed his way to the aisle, tripping and banging against knees in a knot of confusion and grief, and he ran out of the auditorium.

⚬⚬⚬

Grey and dark outside, the start of the long season. Leaning back in his chair with his legs propped on his desk, Sam Jacobson looked out at the snowflakes swirling by his window and the leaves skittering across the street. His office was on the second floor overlooking Chamber Street. The shop below the law office, Ritvo's Antiques, sold vintage clothing and sundries and doubled as the office for a documentary filmmaker.

Merchants came and went in Montpelier. Before the vintage clothing, it had been a store that catered to Wiccans. Sam amused himself with the fantasy of a Wiccan delivering the invocation prayer at the town meeting up in Jefferson where Lucy Cross made her home. And before the Wiccans, he remembered the space had hosted upscale kitchenware, the front window displaying bright-hued colanders and crockery.

On the other hand, Colten's Hardware, around the corner on Sproul Street, was nearing its 80th anniversary, having bravely resisted the box store boom that sought to coat Vermont with a New Jersey pallor, with hardware stores the size of city blocks springing up all over the Champlain Valley. Everybody loved Colten's, where your bill was cranked out of an antique adding machine, and the staff had the facility to advise you precisely what length and girth of bolt you needed for your current home project.

Sam watched the wretched November snow and held both hands around the mug of coffee he had brought back from Sacred Grounds. He thought about Colten's Hardware and then about his wife, Donna, who had a similar kind of stamina, sticking with him through his periods of self-doubt and regret.

They met when he was a law student and she was an undergrad psych major. They had eyed each other on several days over the cheeses at Orange Street Market in New Haven, Connecticut. She spoke the first words, asking him whether he liked manchego. He didn't know what manchego was. She explained about manchego, and the manchega sheep in Spain, although she didn't know, when he asked, just toying with her really, why an Italian market would carry a Spanish sheep cheese.

Sheep and cheese seemed to interest her. It was the way she spoke about sheep and cheese, and the way her calm eyes appraised him as she did so, that interested Sam. They fell in love. They were married three years later, still living in New Haven, and her pregnancy with the child who became Sarah shocked them into moving north to cold, sane Vermont.

He had been ready, anyway, to leave his job as an associate at New Haven's largest law firm, where the leading partner who assigned Sam most of his projects periodically jaunted to Africa for safari hunts. He killed lions, for crying out loud.

Sam stroked the cleft in his chin, the coffee mug set precariously on a stack of files at the edge of the desk. In his mind now, he pictured Donna, over the cheese board on their kitchen table, with her calm blue-grey eyes fixed on him, and her mouth, even and kind.

Suddenly he felt awful he had left the house that morning saying hardly more than two words to Donna. "What's on your agenda for today?" she had asked. "The usual stuff at the office. You?" and he was out the door heading to Sacred Grounds. Her words, "See you tonight at dinner-time," drifted out to the street after him.

He was taking her for granted. He vowed to stop doing that. He tried her cell phone but got no answer. She would be in the car by now, heading to her office in Riverbury. He didn't leave a message.

He'd have to ask Donna about Ricky Stillwell, he thought. Maybe Donna had heard something from Clara. Ricky was acting pretty strange that morning at the café, rushing out in his loping stride— much as Sam had left his house, barely saying a word.

He liked the kid immensely and worried about him. He worried about a lot of things. His prostate, his marriage, Israeli settlements, video games, and Ricky Stillwell.

He didn't worry about the boy's soul, which was surely well protected by virtue of membership in the Fellowship Church of the Crucified Savior, but about his happiness.

He looked at the files piled on the table next to his desk and turned his eyes back to his reading. He was reading a court opinion on the question of whether a bank's security interest in a farmer's cattle also covered the milk and, if so, whether it had priority over the dairy co-op's interest in the milk.

Like Colten's Hardware, the subjects of Vermont case law resisted change. This was one of the things Sam, born and bred in New York City, liked about his adopted state and its legal culture. He read another paragraph, using his yellow highlighter to underline one or another passage. This was performed by habit and served little real function.

The radiator in his office began to clank, and he was startled, glancing its way, to see that Alicia stood at his office door, staring at him.

Alicia Santana had started work as an associate at Sam's office some fifteen years earlier, when there were five lawyers at the firm. Later there was a difficult split, and Sam left with Alicia, who then became his partner. The split had been over personality and money. Sam had come to recognize that it was mostly his personality that was the problem.

That was the way Sam approached the past. He was the villain featured in his autobiographical documentary. And every new year rolled another year into the dreaded past. The list of regrets accumulated, like worn-out furniture in an attic. But he didn't shortchange the future. He worried about that too.

In spite of it all, to his good fortune, and partly by his deft maneuvering, Alicia, high-strung and brilliant, had come with him. He was delighted with the arrangement, and he told himself his delight had nothing to do with her dark sinuous beauty.

The two of them did not always agree. A year or two earlier, Sam had represented one of Montpelier's city councilors who had been the subject of a nasty article in the local paper, *The Central Vermont Argus*. The article asserted that the city councilor had underpaid her federal income tax. But that wasn't true; her taxes had only been filed late, and she had duly requested an extension of time from the IRS. Claiming the newspaper had damaged her reputation by publishing false information, Sam filed a defamation suit.

The case didn't settle and was tried before a jury. The jury found for *The Argus*, on the ground that the newspaper didn't know the information was false at the time it ran the article, nor did it act with "reckless disregard" for the truth of the information, the minimum quantum of fault needed in a case like this, as the judge had instructed and emphasized to the jury. *The Argus* might have been negligent in publishing the article, but negligence was not enough for a public figure like the city councilor to establish liability under the law of defamation.

Sam was angry about the result.

"You shouldn't be suing the press, Sam," Alicia said. "They've got a First Amendment right to publish news stories."

"Fine," said Sam, "but they should take care to get their facts right. This was sloppy reporting."

"You got to live with some slop if you want a free press," she retorted. "They need room to make mistakes. Otherwise, we end up in a police state."

"You're not perhaps overstating things?" Sam suggested.

"No," she said. "I don't want us suing the press."

This sort of disagreement did not trouble Sam. Alicia was at liberty to question his judgment. He knew her objection was a sign of respect. Respect flowed freely between them.

Now she stood in the doorway and stared at Sam with her dark eyes wide. "You haven't heard."

"Heard?" The snow was coming harder outside, moving faster, sideways.

"I just got a call from Barb at the high school," she finally said. "Oh Sam, this is difficult." Alicia's eyes were glistening and she paused again. "The school's in shock."

There was another moment of quiet. "Kerry Pearson is a student there. She's Fran Loughlin's daughter. . . ."

Sam knew of Francine Loughlin, one of the prosecutors at the county State's Attorney's office, and an old friend of Alicia's. Francine and Alicia had been in the same class at Vermont Law School, two women who had bonded together in the tiny community of the law school, laughing and crying about sex and politics, and studying through the night for their exams. Francine's daughter, Kerry, now a senior at Montpelier High School, the same grade as Ricky Stillwell, was still a toddler when her mother and Alicia were in law school, as Sam remembered it, and he knew Alicia had a soft spot for the girl.

Sam nodded. "What happened?"

Alicia looked down for a moment, embarrassed by her tears. "She's dead. Kerry. She committed suicide. Last night I guess. She was found this morning."

Sam took his feet off his desk. His stomach was cramping and the radiator was banging louder. He got up and wrapped his arms around Alicia's small shoulders. She was shaking and could not speak.

The small yellow house on Baker Street confined Francine Loughlin. She wandered about inside the house in her bathrobe, looking for traces of Kerry. She placed one foot before the other. She talked out loud in what sounded like rational sentences as she approached every corner, every doorway in the house, to surmount the terror of what might be on the other side. "There is nothing there," she said, "nothing to be afraid of."

Friends arrived with casseroles. Broccoli and chicken, cheese and noodles. They encouraged Francine to come out. She declined invitations; she was afraid of normal activity and kindnesses. Even Alicia Santana, her exuberant old law school friend, was pushed—politely and gently—from her front porch. Her grief hardened, deep and frozen inside her.

She dwelled on Kerry's last few days. She re-imagined their last breakfast together, toast and peanut butter for Fran, a bowl of Wheat Chex for Kerry, juice for both, a combination of orange and pomegranate. They had prepared their last supper the night before, together as usual. A stir-fry with chicken breast and scallions and fresh kale that Fran could still harvest in November from her garden, the last remaining vegetable. It was not a very special meal.

She saw turmoil in her daughter's face. She did not probe. She thought Kerry would open up to her, as she often did, or would resolve whatever the trouble was on her own, as she sometimes did. Always, always, Kerry had returned to her levelheaded self.

She was a grown-up girl, independent, as if a 30-year-old adult mind inhabited her 17-year-old body. She took calculus a year ahead of her peers, played a strong midfield in lacrosse, listened to Lucinda Williams and Greg Brown instead of the latest pop-tart. It wasn't only Fran who thought her daughter was extraordinary.

Their neighbor on Baker Street, conversing with Francine across the odorous boxwood hedge between their houses, frequently observed that Kerry was a *mensch*. Fran wondered whether a girl could be a mensch. "Why not? Of course," the neighbor had told her, a rake in his calloused hand. "I have watched her for many years. She can do great and good things. She is a true mensch."

"Oh, I know," Fran had said. "Or really I mean to say thank you. I just meant whether the word is used only for males."

"Achh," the neighbor had said. "I use it for whoever earns it. She earns it."

Fran made a cup of Darjeeling tea, in a forlorn effort to thaw her core. The tea brewed and she looked at the photos of Kerry displayed on the fridge, in various happy guises. One showed Kerry, grinning in ski goggles, on a chairlift (was it Jay Peak?), the sun flashing on the goggles, snow sparkling and bright, life sparkling and bright. Kerry's friend Sophie had snapped the photo sitting next to her on the chairlift. Fran stared at it until the sunlight in the photo seared her eyes and she had to look away.

Another photograph showed Kerry and Fran together, arms linked, perched next to a vineyard on a trail overlooking the deep blue Ligurian Sea in Cinque Terre in Italy, where they had toured together, just the two of them, Kerry and her mom, almost a year and a half earlier, feeling the joy of living. Mother and daughter had never been closer.

There, in the vineyard over the blue sea, Kerry told her mom that she really liked other girls, all right, Mom? and she wanted her mom to understand her most important secret—some of the kids at school were so stupid, you know? Oh Kerry, that's fine, that's fine, Fran hollered at her refrigerator door.

She drank the tea and glanced now at the photograph on the fridge door of the varsity lacrosse team, a group of strong athletic girls smiling in the spring sun. The photo was wrinkled and stained where cranberry juice had spilled over it. Kerry stood next to the team's coach, Gayle Peters. Kerry, Francine knew, had liked her coach. More than that, she had once called Peters dazzling. Sure, Fran had thought, the high school principal, a leader, good role model for the girls. But dazzling?

"Yes, Mom," Kerry had told her, "and I'm not the only one," and she named three of her teammates. "Like we all think she's gorgeous. It's like she casts a spell, you know? You should see Sophie with Coach Peters, Mom. Totally possessed!"

Fran didn't understand, didn't see the attraction. No doubt Gayle Peters was a well-respected coach and principal, competent, self-assured, polished. Traits Fran wished she had more of herself, if she were truly honest. As for Sophie, Kerry's friend since third grade, to Fran's eye Sophie seemed smitten by *Kerry* more than anyone else. Sophie always seemed to gaze at Kerry with devoted longing. Maybe Sophie was like that with a lot of people.

On the fridge door below the photographs, under a magnet, was a certificate, signed by Principal Peters, announcing Kerry's induction into the National Honor Society. Her daughter had such unbounded promise and spirit.

When she was a girl of six, Kerry talked with her mother about death. Her father had recently left the marriage and, really, the family, as he moved back to England and stopped communicating with them. Kerry asked if he were dead.

"No, he's just gone away. He's not dead, of course not."

"But he's disappeared, right? Is that dying?"

A year later, their Jack Russell Terrier, who was named Bertrand Russell after the philosopher, but whom Kerry called Bert after the Sesame Street puppet, was killed in front of their house by an errant driver. Kerry was strangely peaceful, though Francine herself was terribly upset. Having heard from friends about heaven, Kerry thought that Bert lived on in a happy place somewhere else, just not visible to them.

Going back even further. Kerry is three. Francine is in her third year of law school, spring semester, the muddy ground of South Royalton drying out in the heat of the spring sun. It is Wednesday afternoon class, no daycare those afternoons. Fran's British husband is off on a work trip as usual. Well, they called it a work trip, but he was doing God knows what, just to get away from Francine, she eventually came to realize.

No daycare, so three-year-old Kerry comes with her mom to the class. It is a class on criminal procedure: *Miranda*, Fourth Amendment searches, due process. Fran's classmate, Alicia Santana, so smart she could blow off lectures, is devoted to Kerry and entertains her by drawing pictures of cows and horses in her notebook. On this one hot Wednesday afternoon, Professor Swain lectures about a case involving a rape and murder of a woman.

Classroom windows are open to the breeze. There are constitutional issues about the police having searched the suspect's friend's apartment without anyone's consent and without a warrant. Alicia is huddled next to Kerry in the back row and they are drawing pictures. Professor Swain is talking. Kerry is not supposed to be listening to the lecture. Of *course* not.

After class, walking across the Green with Fran and Alicia, Kerry stops at a muddy spot and says with a frown on her little face, "If you are killed like that girl in the class, I will be sad. And Alicia will take care of me."

Beautiful Alicia.

Dead Kerry.

The empty frozen hole in her core throbbed. Death, she thought, is permanent and banal. What survives our earthly life is nothing other than memories and objects, treasures or trinkets. Francine wished she could believe there was more to it than that, something transcendent, as Kerry had once believed in their terrier Bert's continued sojourn on another plane.

"I'm sorry," she said to the empty room.

And Francine dwelled, of course, on the question of suicide. The police said that's what had happened. Barry LaPorte, the big sweet man who was paying her so much attention these terrible days: he said that's what happened.

Could it be? Impossible.

Depressives died by suicide when the pain of life became unbearable, but Kerry did not suffer from depression. Surely not? Or might she have encountered some terror from which flight by suicide was the rational response? Or faced a tragic choice, where a life continued was a morally worse outcome than death?

People did choose death. Socrates chose death over forsaking his deep principles. Mohamed Bouazizi chose death on a Tunisian street as a final burning statement of anguish and protest, igniting the Arab Spring. What could possibly have driven Kerry to a cliff's edge in Mahady Park?

At that point in her spiraling ruminations Francine made the decision to tackle what she had put off. Kerry's laptop was sitting there on the kitchen table.

Fran opened it and went to Kerry's emails. In the Inbox and Sent Items from two weeks before, and earlier in a folder labeled Dears, Fran found emails with Kerry's friends Sophie and Amanda. She read, feeling the sickness of a voyeur.

The exchanges were innocuous for the most part. One was interesting. Kerry had written: "Things are hard right now. I am growing, learning, expanding! I hope not exploding! I need to step back." Sophie: "From what?" Amanda: "What RU talking about?" Kerry: "I can't really say. I'll be all right. Your friendship is my solid earth." Fran whispered an echo to the screen, "What RU talking about?"

Kerry could not answer.

Then Fran opened Facebook; Kerry's password was pre-programmed and her "news feed" appeared on the screen. Several friends had posted their thoughts following Kerry's death. Fran scanned the sad material, grief and pathos in equal measure. Two or three friends asked the question of Why Did This Happen, but no one responded with an intelligible explanation.

For a while Fran bounced around the site, scanning the list of friends, following this or that link. She finished the tea. She felt hopeless.

She clicked on the Message icon. This is the place on Facebook where you can send private messages that are not posted for others to see. There was a message from Ricky Stillwell. Francine knew of Ricky as Kerry's classmate. She remembered some story that Ricky had espoused fundamentalist religious opinions, and she had wondered whether his faith was what her daughter had admired, in spite of their differences.

Fran stared at the page and read the top message out loud.

SORRY! PLEASE MEET ME TOMORROW
AT 3 AT SACRED GROUNDS.

Just below that was another message, sent two hours earlier.

KERRY, HOMOSEXUALITY IS A SIN
AGAINST GOD. IT IS PERVERSION
AGAINST THE NATURAL ORDER. MAYBE
YOU SHOULD BE OUTED AND THE
WHOLE SCHOOL WILL KNOW.

Fran gulped for air and her throat burned. She wheeled around, lurched to the kitchen sink, and threw up. She wiped her face and walked into the living room and sat down on the birch rocker next to the woodstove. She pulled her knees up and tucked her feet under her and wrapped her arms around her legs to keep herself from coming apart. She heard the word perversion in the air around her.

After a time she called the police sergeant. "Please, Barry, can you come here? I want to show you what I found."

"What is it, Fran, what happened?" he asked.

"I'm at my house. I'm sorry to be needy. Will you come?"

It is the policy of the state of Vermont
that all Vermont educational institutions provide safe,
orderly, civil and positive learning environments.
Harassment, hazing and bullying
have no place and will not be tolerated in
Vermont schools. No Vermont student should feel
threatened or be discriminated against while
enrolled in a Vermont school.

Title 16, Vermont Statutes Annotated, § 570(a)

Severe and determined, Principal Gayle Peters paced around her office. Superintendent Allen Bird, watching her, was reminded of a caged big cat. On speakerphone was the school district's counsel, Tad Sorowski. Tad was short for Tadeusz. Barb Laval, as usual, was present.

Peters was emphatic. "We can't let this drop. This young man, Ricky Stillwell, well, you know what kind of harm comes from these things he said online. He harassed Kerry Pearson. My God, he's the one responsible for her killing herself." She paused to assess, with her hand held midair. "At some level."

And, before anyone could interject, "And I don't care if his mother is on the school board."

"I think you do have authority to punish Stillwell under section 570 of Title 16 and board policy." Sorowski was speaking. "What the young man did here constitutes harassment; he made intimidating statements based on another student's sexual orientation."

Allen Bird, the superintendent, was hesitant. "But he didn't write this stuff at school as far as we know. This was on his own computer. Tad, can you tell us whether this is a problem?"

Peters stopped in front of her boss, still agitated. "Allen, it's all about school. Ricky's a student here; Kerry was a student here. They knew each other through school. He threatened to expose her at school. He's a danger to others. It shouldn't matter *where* he made his slurs. This sort of behavior is grounds for expulsion."

The principal kept toys in her office, and now she picked one from the book shelf, a tiny green plastic Godzilla-like creature with a key on its back. Peters wound the key and set the creature on the table. It marched forward for five or six steps with a loud buzzing sound, and fell off the edge of the table to the floor, where it buzzed for another few seconds. Peters bent down and reached for the creature.

Superintendent Bird watched her and thought there was something manic about the principal's actions. She was moving too quickly, was too distracted. When she glanced up at him as she grabbed the plastic creature, she grinned in a way he felt did not fit the mood. But perhaps she was just covering her embarrassment over the silliness with Godzilla.

Unlike the others at this meeting, Bird knew something of Peters's medical file and a period of opiate addiction in her twenties that had come to light when she applied for the principal's job. But there had been no recurrence, as far as he knew. Until this moment it hadn't occurred to him that she might still have an addiction problem. Normally she was cool and confident.

The attorney, Sorowski, spoke from the phone. "Allen, I think the connection between Ricky Stillwell's message and the school is sufficiently strong. The school may penalize a student for disseminating writings from a source outside school when they are designed or likely to affect the learning and disciplinary environment within the school." Impeccable but pedantic diction, as always with Tad Sorowski.

"But do we face legal exposure," Bird asked again, "if we punish this kid for what he said? Doesn't the First Amendment limit our options?"

Bird wondered too how Clara Stillwell would react. She was a conservative Christian who probably encouraged—for all he knew even tutored—Ricky in his homophobic views. A school board member, she was his boss, and Peters's boss too. Or, rather, one of several.

"Ah, you cannot stop someone from bringing suit," said Sorowski. "You are always exposed in that sense. That does not mean you are exposed to significant risk of liability. Almost certainly, you, as individual administrators, would be immune from any monetary liability, because the law in this area is not well established."

Public officials were personally exposed to legal liability only when their actions violated clearly established law. Then Sorowski added with his usual caution, "But could the school district as an institution be faced with liability? I think not, but possibly so. I cannot be certain. There are competing values at stake: on the one hand, the constitutional right of free speech; on the other, the district's authority and obligation to provide a safe learning environment free of harassment of vulnerable persons. There are no guarantees as to how that conflict will resolve."

This lawyerly response hardly satisfied an uneasy Superintendent Bird. He leaned back in his chair and held his hands together before him in a prayerful posture. Gayle Peters had finally taken a seat during Sorowski's speech. She cranked the key on Godzilla's back, and once more let the monster free on the table, where it marched in its jerky stride and stopped, depleted, in the middle, while Bird and Barb Laval watched. Sorowski, on the speakerphone, said, "What is happening in there? I hear an unusual sound."

"It's Godzilla," replied Bird.

"You're speaking now of our good principal?" said Sorowski, with rare humor.

"I think he should be expelled," Gayle Peters repeated, all business.

She turned to Barb Laval, tucked inside her enormous sweater. "Can you tell us whether he still needs credits to graduate? What's his status?"

At the computer on the principal's desk, Barb retrieved Ricky Stillwell's student file. She conveyed the essentials. There were some moments of confusion about gym credits. Once that was sorted out, they concluded that Ricky had not yet garnered the credits required for a high school diploma, but all he needed to do was to complete the current fall semester courses. He would then have sufficient credits to graduate.

They reached an accommodation under Superintendent Bird's guidance: the school would let Ricky Stillwell work from home to finish up his fall course load, take the exams, and be done by the end of January. Assuming he passed the courses, which no one doubted, he could get his diploma. But he would not be permitted back in school, from this day forward.

No spring classes, no sports or extra-curriculars, no participation in graduation exercises. *Persona non grata.* The plan satisfied Peters. She would bring the proposal to the school board. Stillwell would be on short-term suspension until the board could meet and act.

A week later, Ricky Stillwell and his parents had a difficult meeting with Principal Peters and Superintendent Bird around the table in the principal's office. Ricky said nothing during the entire meeting. He sat awkwardly, stared at Peters and stared at his feet, and gritted his teeth, the bones of his jaw shifting visibly below his skin.

His mother, Clara, sitting forward and erect in her seat, argued her son's case, but without Ricky's participation there would certainly be no change of heart by the school administrators. Ricky was cast out.

Sarah Jacobson drove up to Vermont from Providence for Thanksgiving with her folks. She had borrowed her friend William's 1986 Toyota with a bad muffler and a missing front passenger window, the space now covered with plastic and duct tape. The loud snapping of the plastic as she drove made her jittery. Too much coffee contributed.

Sarah felt ambivalent about the holiday because she thought it celebrated a meeting of cultures that masked incipient genocide of native peoples. And turkey disgusted her, especially its pimply skin. But she did usually enjoy her occasional sojourns north from Rhode Island to come home to Montpelier.

Sarah was immersed in her work and her world and she felt, most of the time, she could safely ignore her parents because they were so *established*. She lived alone in a second-floor apartment in a neighborhood of Guatemalan and Dominican immigrants (or migrants, as Sarah insisted on saying). She split her workday between two community nonprofits, organizing campaigns that currently focused on labor abuses and foreclosures.

She walked into the kitchen unannounced and found her father pouring a can of coconut milk into the curry simmering on the stove. For Sarah's benefit, he had promised to use tofu rather than meat, and vegetable broth rather than chicken stock, and no Thai fish sauce. Aromas of coriander and cumin rose from the pot.

He put the can down and gave his daughter an earnest hug. Donna, fixing a beet salad, dropped the knife on the cutting board and clasped Sarah around her shoulders. "Oh honey, you made it home. Was the drive okay?"

In the living room, Sarah soon spread out on the sofa with a recent *New York Review of Books*, reading a retrospective review of the work of historian Tony Judt, who had died a few years ago from Lou Gehrig's disease. But the prose was too thick and she was tired. She clicked on the TV, where a senator was speaking to journalist Judy Woodruff. Sarah caught a snatch of topical idiom erupting into a perfect storm of cliché—"will be a game-changer if he doubles down and we'll have to go it alone"— before she shut it off and yelled, "Like clichés on steroids!" adding one more tired phrase to the noxious brew as she threw the remote onto the sofa.

She wandered back to the kitchen in a sour mood. Sarah had the keen blueish eyes and firm jaw of her mother and the mess of curls and propensity to irritation of her father.

She stuck her nose in the pot and gathered in the rich scents. She cast a sardonic eye at her father, who had asked as she wandered in, "What are you growling about now, Sarahkins?"

Sarah ignored this and said instead, "Meg called me, Dad."

Meg Stillwell, Sarah's long-time friend, was Ricky's older sister, who now lived with her boyfriend in Seattle, a stone's throw from Gas Works Park. Meg was a manager at the Wallingford Food Coop. The boyfriend, Matthew Einstein-Moomjy, played keyboards and ultimate Frisbee, or one of its spin-offs. Sarah had met him once when she went out to Seattle to visit Meg.

They had gone to a bar where they listened to spoken poetry in a hip hop vein, delivered by a Russian immigrant with keyboard accompaniment by the versatile Matthew. At some point in the evening Sarah could see that Meg and Matthew were eyeing each other. The vibe of the bar room eventually led to the deeper groove of cohabitation and much else. Meg's parents, the infamous Clara and Carver, did not know about Matthew Einstein-Moomjy. Better that way.

"How is Meg doing?" Sam asked his daughter. "Is she home for the holiday?"

"No, she's staying in Seattle. And how do you think she's doing?" Sarah was still affronted by the drivel on TV, and now her father was being clueless. "She's a mess. Her brother's become a nut job. Your protégé." She grimaced in her father's direction. "He's like as wacky as Clara. Meg told me about the stuff he posted about that girl on Facebook."

"Oh, I know. It's terrible, Sarah. It is hard to believe Ricky wrote what he did." But he reconsidered as he adjusted the flame under the simmering rice. "No, that's not really true. I've heard him say things a bit like that before. But not quite in that way. About this. About her."

He spooned out a bit of the curry, blew on it, and tasted, and tried to make his thoughts more coherent. "But, Sarah, don't blame Ricky too much. Kerry Pearson committed suicide. Ricky couldn't know."

"You think so?" she said with a sarcastic drip.

"He couldn't know how she'd react. I mean, of course what he wrote was awful and painful. There's a lot of pain everywhere. I don't really know Francine Loughlin that well—she's Kerry's mother—but Alicia is close to her. Alicia says she is destroyed by this. Well, of course." He looked at his daughter. "Some things you can't help."

She stared back at him. Ricky could damn well have helped, she thought.

"I mean, it is what it is," he added idiotically.

"*It is what it is*? Don't be lame, Dad. You sound like John McCain on the TV just now. What does that mean? That no one is responsible for anything? That it's *fate*, for Christ's sake, or providence?" said the girl who lived in Providence.

It was as if Sarah were channeling her father's voice from an incident years in the past. They were in the Ford minivan, on the way to a soccer game in Northwood, some fifteen miles south of Montpelier. Sarah and Meg, who must have been about twelve, were in the back seat.

Clara Stillwell sat in the front of the van while Sam drove, the man on the radio talking about the recent abduction, rape and murder of a local girl by her uncle. Clara made some comment about the crime, which Sarah had forgotten, but Clara ended it with words Sarah did remember. "There's a reason for everything," Clara had intoned.

This is the kind of thing people say without thought, Sarah understood. But Clara had uttered the words with intention and her manner conveyed her fervent belief. Clara was known for this.

From her rear seat, Sarah saw her father stiffen and his knuckles tighten on the wheel. She caught a glimpse of his face in the rearview mirror, fury in his eyes. Then her father bit his words through clenched teeth. "I suppose there's a reason for every horror—for the destruction of the Jews of Europe? It was all meant to happen? It's all fate, just deserts, all God's will? What the hell."

The minivan swerved precariously across the yellow line— at least as Sarah recalled. Clara had no answer. Meg had only looked out the window and would not meet Sarah's eye.

Here in the family kitchen, with the curry aromas in the air, the memory of the incident flooded Sarah's mind, and she felt utter intolerance of her father's obtuseness about Ricky's moral responsibility.

Sam remembered the incident too, but he remembered it differently. He remembered feeling disgust, not anger. He was driving their minivan—Donna's and his minivan—

to bring the girls to the Northwood soccer match, on a warm
October day, with Clara riding up front. Donna was—where
was Donna?—perhaps at work, or maybe at that aromatherapy
class she took back then.

On the car radio was the terrible murder of the girl by
her uncle, and Clara looked over at Sam in the driver's seat,
nodded her head in her solemn way, and said, "Such a horrible
thing to happen to an innocent girl. But there's a reason for
everything."

"What the hell," said Sam, feeling disgust—disgust to the
point it made his gut cramp up. There was no *reason*, he wanted
to cry out, no reason whatsoever for this child's violent death
at the hands and pelvis of her demented uncle, no reason in the
teleological sense. An explanation perhaps, fault for sure, but
no reason—no purpose, or end. Clara spoke as if the girl were
punished because it was her *due*.

"Do you really mean to say," he had asked Clara in an
ugly tone, "you think there's a reason for every atrocity,
like there is a reason the Jews were murdered by the Nazis?
A *reason*? Part of God's plan? Is that the kind of God you
believe in?"

And Clara, this woman for whom he sometimes felt such
affinity and warmth, answered him simply and astonishingly,
"Yes." She believed in a God whose plan included the murder
of six million Jews, including Sam's relatives, for a reason—but
we are not equipped to divine what the reason is. Only that it
was meant to be.

He wanted to vomit.

As for the minivan crossing the center line as Sarah recalled,
that certainly never happened, not the way Sam remembered
it. He was agitated but steady, disgusted by Clara's arrogant
fervor, and he shut the radio off and inserted a cassette tape of
Dylan's album *Desire*, and Dylan was wailing about his love as
they drove on into Northwood.

That was the memory that came back to him as his daughter chastised him for insulating Ricky Stillwell from responsibility for Kerry Pearson's death.

Donna would later tell him as they went to bed that she also recalled the story, because she had heard it from Sam, not from Sarah, so many years ago. What she recalled was the feeling of regret, that Sam felt regret that he had hurt Clara's feelings, as he told Donna the evening after the Northwood soccer match, by mocking Clara's views about fate and God's plan. As usual, Sam was beating himself up.

"No, of course it wasn't fate, Sarah," said Sam now in their Montpelier kitchen as he reached up to return the herb jars to their slots in the rack above the stove. He rubbed his chin, itching to tug at the beard that was no longer there. He faced his disgruntled daughter. "So you're right. I just mean Kerry's suicide wasn't Ricky's fault. He was venting his fundamentalist ideas, and Kerry reacted unpredictably. We don't always *know*." Sam felt himself on shaky ground.

Donna came and stood beside Sarah and touched her cheek, silently establishing that her own daughter was right here, alive, in the flesh, in the kitchen. Sarah understood the intent, and gently kissed her mother's forehead. "I know, Mom," she said, then turned to Sam.

"Dad, they weren't just ideas, like some intellectual game. The way I heard it, Ricky threatened to out the girl. Kerry? Right? He was messing with stuff that wasn't his business."

"He was," Sam told his daughter, "acting out of love."

"Oh? How on earth do you come to that conclusion? It was hate speech, not love speech."

He could see that she now felt he was patronizing her. Old buttons.

Sam wasn't certain about what motivated Ricky Stillwell, and his own words had surprised him. But he knew about Ricky's passionate will, his belief he had a mandate from God directing him to hold his fellows to their best selves, to hold them accountable—out of love. Sam wished, sometimes, that he could have a similar rectitude.

❧

December passed. A new year began. The suicide of Kerry Pearson hung cold over Montpelier like the accumulating snow on the surrounding hills.

Up in Jefferson Center, hard on the Canadian border, the ailing nonagenarian pacifist Lucy Cross was holed up, kept inside by the ice on the walk and her rheumatism and the subzero temperatures. And by the coldness of her neighbors, all good Christians, who had shunned her ever since she stood up at town meeting to object to the traditional prayer, and shunned her even more when, after four years of futile protestations, she had filed suit against her town.

Her neighbors, all good Christians, voted her down four times at town meeting and wrote letters to *The Agrarian Sentinel*, the local paper, exposing her ignominy. She was called, by one of the neighbor letter writers, a "bimbo," a nice demonstration of the mysterious power of misogyny to creep uninvited into an unrelated conversation.

Several writers kindly advised Lucy to move away from Jefferson, leave the country, and find a home in the "Third World," or in a "totalitarian country," where her intolerant views would be welcomed. They urged her to change her name. "You're not worthy," one wrote, "of the name Cross. You should be named Trident!" Such were the puzzling speculations and suggestions offered to resolve the challenges posed by Lucy Cross. As it was, in fact, she couldn't even leave her house, a small cape, white clapboard with grey trim, tucked up next to the United Church and the village green, a short walk from Morse's Country Store.

Sam Jacobson, meanwhile, worked on his Second Circuit appeal brief on the case. Lucy Cross had stood firm, trying to keep official religion out of her town meeting, and for doing her conscientious duty she was ostracized from the public square. Like a student expelled from high school, Sam thought. He would use the courts, he hoped, to redeem her troubles at least. This was the promise of the law in its best light.

But it was an uphill battle. Thomas Jefferson's wall of separation between church and state had become a porous boundary. Courts around the country upheld prayers in diverse civic contexts—state legislative sessions, city council meetings, school board hearings—as permissible "acknowledgments of our religious tradition." Or the courts justified public prayers as manifestations of "ceremonial deism."

That was the label employed to provide constitutional legitimacy to the nation's motto *In God We Trust* stamped on every coin and bill, and to the words *under God* added to the Pledge of Allegiance in the McCarthy era to demonstrate to the Communists how superior we God-fearing Americans were.

Sam was afraid he and Lucy would lose the appeal. Lucy Cross had such faith in him, but he worried he would let her down. True to his morose self, Sam wondered too whether a legal victory for Lucy would lead only to the perverse result of fanning greater hostility in the reaches of Jefferson Center. You lose some, you lose some.

Alicia Santana once asked him why he had taken this *pro bono* case. "No, no," she stopped him when he began with an homage to the First Amendment. "I know this is about defending freedom of conscience under the First Amendment. Of *course*. That's the legal argument. Government and religion don't mix, *et cetera*. But aren't you after something else, too?"

Alicia rushed emphatically forward with her usual verbal vigor. "I mean, Sam, aren't you also saying we ought to keep religion out of the town meeting, not *just* because public officials shouldn't impose their religious views under the First Amendment, but also because, well, you know . . ."—now stopping for the briefest moment, reluctant even to voice the heretical notion—"religion is a bad idea, a form of mass delusion? Opiate of the people, right? It's cosmological rubbish, false science—the miracles, divine creation, virgin birth, walking on water, heaven and hell, the whole enchilada. Plus, it's homophobic. *Hello?* Let's just say it, for Christ's sake." Alicia stopped to breathe.

"You're an atheist, Alicia?" Sam peered over his glasses at his good friend and partner at law. "I guess we've never quite had this discussion."

"I come out of one closet at a time," she said, and threw him her incandescent grin. "Well?" she asked, when he just looked at her with his dopey smile in return.

"I don't know, maybe. That's not the legal analysis. I'm definitely not saying *that* publicly."

"You're a spineless piece of shit," she said.

Far from the Canadian border, seventy miles south as the crow flies, in the grand metropolis of Montpelier, the Stillwells too remained confined, like Lucy Cross and Francine Loughlin. Carver retreated deeper into his silent workshop of tools and wood shavings. Clara hovered between work and home and felt bitter and brittle. If she ventured out in Montpelier, she felt exposed to scorn, imagining cold shoulders turned her way.

No callers offered the Stillwells meals and love. Though she still found respite in her church, Clara felt indelibly torn from her community. Her daughter Meg, living in Seattle, kept her emotional distance. Phone conversation with her was strained and studded with awkward silences, leaving them all feeling worse. The one mitigating fact was that Ricky had managed to gain admission to New York University in the fall. But even that development was, she feared, only a sign that Ricky was devolving away from the church.

From these recesses, Clara Stillwell made an appointment with Sam Jacobson. For years, he had shared an unusual bond with Ricky. Watching them together, gleefully sparring about religion and law, she had felt a mixture of pleasure and horror, pride and jealousy.

Now Sam, her atheist Jewish friend and adversary, who had once taken care of her when she drove off the road on a cold winter night, was one of the few souls she could turn to. She had a legal question. "Do we have a case?" she asked. "Ricky tells me he's another *Tinker*."

Part II
Stillwell's Armband

Any departure from absolute regimentation may cause trouble. Any variation from the majority's opinion may inspire fear. Any word spoken, in class, in the lunchroom, or on the campus, that deviates from the views of another person may start an argument or cause a disturbance. But our Constitution says we must take this risk; and our history says that it is this sort of hazardous freedom—this kind of openness—that is the basis of our national strength and of the independence and vigor of Americans who grow up and live in this relatively permissive, often disputatious, society.

Tinker v. Des Moines Independent Community School District, 393 U.S. 503, 508-509 (1969) (citation omitted)

Alicia Santana sat up straight with a pile of photocopied court opinions on her lap and grinned at Sam Jacobson. "Sam, let me lay it out for you." She faced him from the chair on the other side of his desk, her face bright. "From the beginning."

Sam looked gratefully at his partner, whose passion for legal argument was infectious. "The Supreme Court has dealt with student speech in public schools in just a handful of cases," she began. "It starts with *Tinker*. Students were suspended from school because they wore black armbands to protest the war in Vietnam. It's 1965. The court ruled that the school violated the kids' First Amendment rights. Students in public school have a First Amendment right to speak. Here's the famous phrase. Students don't 'shed their constitutional rights to freedom of speech or expression at the schoolhouse gate.' That's the foundation."

Sam was, of course, familiar with the seminal case. He interrupted Alicia to test his understanding: "Unless the speech is disruptive, right? I mean, a teacher can stop a kid from yelling out nonsense in class. It's not like the proverbial soap box in the town square." Where people yell out nonsense all the time, he didn't need to add.

"Exactly, Sam. Schools are not town squares. They have some latitude to suppress student speech. The standard in *Tinker* is that the school administrators, before they muzzle a student, must be able to show that the student's speech is likely to disrupt, substantially disrupt, school programs, or that it will interfere with the rights of other students. Disruption or interference, either one. Although, you know, the subsequent cases aren't always clear that it's disjunctive."

Alicia's leg was vibrating under her chair. "You can't ban speech at school just because it makes others *uncomfortable*. Okay? Discomfort's not enough. Speech that might provoke an argument is not enough. Substantial disruption and interference are. That'll be the test for Ricky's case."

Sam nodded.

He thought how, at their meeting the previous Thursday, Clara Stillwell's vehemence had made *him* uncomfortable. On the other hand, Ricky seemed uncertain, to the point of being mysterious, and conflicted about the idea of bringing a lawsuit. Sam had not promised to take the case. "Let me think about it and do some research," he had told them.

Alicia now smiled at him. "Put aside the narrow circumstances in which a school can limit a student's speech, just for a moment, Sam."

"Okay," he said.

"This case, Sam, stands for a beautiful, expansive vision of the First Amendment," Alicia went on. "The strength of our nation, the *Tinker* court says, lies in our open society, our disputatious society. We have to nourish and protect what the court called the *hazardous* freedom endowed to us by the Constitution. Can you believe it?"

Sam said, "Hardly."

"Man, the rhetoric in *Tinker* is so rich, Sam. You can't imagine a Supreme Court case with language like that today. Justice Fortas—he wrote the majority opinion in 1969—even offered this little treasure: 'In our system, state-operated schools may not be enclaves of totalitarianism.'"

"He wrote that?" asked Sam.

"He did," she said. "So a school that suppresses a student's political speech is behaving like Nazi Germany or the USSR! And then Fortas wrote that students 'may not be confined to the expression of those sentiments that are officially approved.' These radical words! It's strong stuff, Sam. The court today is a shrunken vestige of what it once was."

"Ah, the times they are a-changin'," was Sam's contribution.

Alicia tolerated him happily. "The second Supreme Court case," she continued, coming down a register, "is *Bethel School District versus Fraser* in 1986. A kid there made a speech at a school assembly trying to get his buddy elected to head the student council or something, and his speech was totally sexual, full of innuendo. All about an erection."

She smiled at Sam as if inviting him to just try and produce one. She charged forward. "So the court added to *Tinker*, or subtracted from *Tinker* is maybe a better way to say it, and held that school officials could take steps to protect students—even high school students—from sexually explicit speech. This wasn't based on any showing of substantial disruption. It's an independent ground for suppressing speech.'"

Sam held his hand up for a second, almost asking for permission to slow Alicia down. "I don't think Ricky's Facebook message," he said, "would be thought of as sexual, other than using the word homosexual. The *Bethel* case doesn't apply—you agree?"

"Right. I agree. Now, in 2007 the court limited *Tinker* further in the "Bong Hits" case, *Morse* versus Frederick."

Sam nodded, remembering the case.

"High school students are out on the street, during the school day—the school's allowed it—to watch the Olympic Torch Relay go by. And one of the kids, this guy Frederick, somehow takes out this 14-foot banner that says in big letters, BONG HiTS 4 JESUS"—Alicia spelled it out—"and he unfurls it before national TV cameras. Unbelievable stunt. The court ends up saying," and Alicia shuffled the pages to find the highlighted quote, "that 'schools may take steps to safeguard those entrusted to their care from speech that can reasonably be regarded as encouraging illegal drug use.' Wow. If the speech somehow encourages drug use, the school can suppress it, again *regardless* of the *Tinker* standard. You don't need to show disruption."

"Okay, Alicia—and?" Where was she going?

"And Justice Sam Alito wrote a concurring opinion. Let me tell you what Alito wrote." Alicia was buzzing. "He says he joined the majority opinion *only* on the understanding," and Alicia again turned to the document to find the quote, "that '(a) it goes no further than to hold that a public school may restrict speech that a reasonable observer would interpret as advocating illegal drug use and (b) it provides no support for any restriction of speech that can possibly be interpreted as commenting on any political or social issue.' It's the second part that's critical for us: Alito makes this bold declaration that the court must not be understood as endorsing any limitation on student speech that can *possibly* be interpreted"—Alicia vibrating faster every time she emphasized a word—"as *commenting* on a political or social issue."

"Good. Fine. That's good for Ricky's case. He was commenting on a social issue." At their meeting with the Stillwells, that's more or less what Ricky had said, that he knew he was in a tiny minority in the Montpelier community, and he wanted to speak up about his views. He wanted to tell his friend Kerry what he thought about her sexual "choices"—his word—which he characterized as a religious issue.

Sure, Sam had thought, but did you have to threaten Kerry in the process?

MAYBE YOU SHOULD BE OUTED AND THE WHOLE SCHOOL WILL KNOW.

Alicia leaned her slender frame forward and looked at Sam. "What Alito's really about is this: Sure, he obviously thought young Mr. Frederick could be punished for the Bong Hits banner because of the drug thing. But there's more behind this. It's a play in the culture wars. Alito's underlying objective is to use First Amendment doctrine to preserve *religious* speech from what he thinks of as politically correct attempts to suppress it."

Sam lost the thread here. "But Alicia, *Morse* is about drugs, not religion." He felt stupid.

"I know, I know. But that's why he was so insistent on *limiting* the holding in *Morse*. It's not just Alito's concurrence in *Morse v. Frederick*. There's a back story here. Before he got put on the Supreme Court, you know, he sat on the Third Circuit Court of Appeals. In 2001 he wrote the opinion for that court in a case called *Saxe v. State College Area School District*.

This school district in Pennsylvania had an anti-harassment policy—by and large like the policy adopted in Montpelier—and Alito held that it violated the First Amendment."

Alicia was grinning again. "The case, Sam, involved *Christian* students who wanted to speak out about how sinful *homosexuality* was. Sound familiar?"

Sam nodded obediently.

"The students sued, claiming they feared they would be punished under the school's harassment policy. And Alito agreed with the students. He ruled that the policy basically barred too much speech. Right? He said the school's harassment policy was so broad it would cover any speech about a person's characteristics that merely *offended* someone, like talking about someone's religious traditions or about sexual orientation. That's why the policy had to be struck down."

She stopped to catch her breath.

"You see? You get it? Alito's on a campaign to protect Christians, like the students in the *Saxe* case, who believe in *traditional* values." Her fingers made air quotes. "The students have the constitutional right to call homosexuality a sin. They have that right, that freedom of speech. Justice Alito is brandishing the First Amendment like a shield, holding it up against liberal elites who, in Alito's tortured mind, want to muzzle conservative Christians by enforcing school speech codes. He despises liberals. That's where the court is moving, Sam. We can win this case."

"I suppose the rest of the right flank is with Alito on this?"

"It's not that clear. Only Kennedy joined Alito's opinion in *Morse v. Frederick*. Roberts wrote the majority opinion that Alito was concurring with—which, you know, ruled *against* Frederick's right to display his bizarre banner. It is *not* a speech-protective opinion, right? As for Justice Thomas, he's out there in Neverland, in the other direction from Alito entirely. Ha! He thinks public school students don't have free speech rights, period. Schools act in the role of parents and the Constitution does not constrain them. Thomas wrote a separate concurring opinion in *Morse v. Frederick*. Nobody joined him. He'd out and out overrule *Tinker*."

Clarence Thomas, of all the justices, paid the least tribute to *stare decisis*, respect for precedents, Sam knew. "Why am I not surprised," he said. "So we press Alito's view of the First Amendment?"

"That's right, we *do*. Oh, Sam, I've had stranger bedfellows." Another salacious grin.

Not for the first time, Sam wondered for a distracted moment how it would be to lie down with Alicia, to feel her lips on his, to run his hands along her flat belly, to be her bedfellow. He tried to banish the thought.

He had talked with Donna about these feelings on more than one occasion, because she had asked him directly. Alicia was that striking. Donna was patient with him on this subject, in part because there seemed to be little risk of any overt transgression in view of Alicia's present inclinations. Alicia herself had obliquely told Sam that she had no interest in a romantic relationship with anyone other than Barb Laval. She just had a way with words and gestures that aroused the appetites.

As for Sam and Donna, their marital history was not entirely monogamous, going back to the early years anyway, a bit of a sore point for Donna. She too fell in love with others, men and women both; that was not the issue. Donna's expression of love did not require sex as an essential ingredient. Sam, on the other hand, could not separate the parts. He always answered her questions truthfully, but usually did not volunteer information of this type. Such was the balance they had struck. He would tell the truth and nothing but the truth, but would not agree that he was compelled to tell the *whole* truth.

In the late 1990s, before the firm split up, Sam had served occasionally as a hearing officer for the Vermont Department of

Banking and Insurance, and in that capacity was called upon to swear in witnesses. Most hearing officers and judges posed the usual performative query to witnesses, which invoked religious scruples as a test of the witness's commitment to veracity: *Do you solemnly swear that the evidence you shall give in the matter now under consideration shall be the truth, the whole truth, and nothing but the truth, so help you God?*

In accordance with his irreligious scruples, Sam substituted the word *affirm* for the word *swear,* dropped the final reference to the deity, and added in its stead the permissible secular alternative: *under the pains and penalties of perjury.* And then he made one additional alteration to the witness query. Sam dropped the words *the whole truth* because, truth be told, who could ever really tell the whole truth? It was just too big.

Just so, Sam believed he could not tell the whole truth to Donna or to anyone else about his heart and its attachments. But when she did ask about Alicia—"Sam, with all these late nights at the office recently, can I just ask, are you *acting* on your attraction to Alicia?"—he could and did answer. "No, no, I don't think she has any interest in that whatsoever, and I probably wouldn't anyway." The truth and nothing but.

The same rules held fast now, though Alicia, sitting on the opposite side of his office desk, looked especially incandescent as she propagated her legal polemics. "I've got more to share," Alicia said, interrupting Sam's reverie.

She stood up and banged her stack of papers into alignment. "There's a bunch of cases dealing with the problem of punishing student speech that emanates from a home computer rather than occurring in the school itself. The question there is whether speech should be *more* protected, whether the *Tinker* exception even applies. But none of those cases are at the Supreme Court level. Can it wait 'til Monday? I'm in depositions all day tomorrow in the Cusick case and I've got tons to prepare."

Sam nodded. "Alicia, before you go. So, okay, you've

framed the argument. I think the analysis makes sense. I think I get it. You've explained it well. But, Alicia, should we take the case? I mean, how do you feel about it?"

"Defending Ricky? The weird thing, Sam, is I haven't thought about that. That's your call. He's your buddy, right? I like him, whatever his views. For me, I just see this as a First Amendment problem, and I've given you the First Amendment analysis. A student is speaking to another student about sexuality and God, and the school wants to censor him. No, no, no."

She left his office, and as her glow receded, Sam was left to wonder why he should want to promote Samuel Alito's vision of the Constitution by defending Ricky's anti-gay rant. Glancing through the window to Chamber Street below, he watched a male couple, holding hands and leaning in together, as they waited in the slush for the light to change at the corner of Sproul Street.

Sam went to bed early, reading another Colin Dexter mystery with Inspector Morse chewing out Lewis, as usual. Donna climbed in next to him, and after a few moments without his acknowledging her, she turned out the light. He grumbled about wanting to finish the paragraph, but when she wrapped a leg over his, he maneuvered her head into the space between his shoulder and grizzled cheek, smelling her hair, while he put his hand on her bottom. They breathed together.

Then he said: "Nice dinner you made tonight. I love those little potatoes."

He was, she knew, inviting a conversation. "Yes, they were good," she told him. "I used butter." She smiled, remembering that she had told him on occasion not to use butter for one thing or another. He stayed silent and she added, "Butter and some of those French herbs. Herbes de Provence. You like?"

Sam moved his head up and down and patted her bottom.

Changing tone, Donna said, "It seems like it's been a while since we sat down together for a real dinner. When you're not watching the Newshour, or heading out to a meeting, or whatever."

"I know," he said, and waited in the darkness for Donna to continue.

"You do seem preoccupied, Sam."

"Well, *yeah*," he said childishly with an accent of sarcasm on the second word.

"What about?"

"I guess it's Ricky's case. It's awfully perplexing. I'm wondering whether I should have taken it on."

Of course, she thought. Donna didn't know legal doctrine. She followed the human story, glossing over abstractions of the law, classifications, levels of scrutiny. She was a vocational counselor. "Why did you?"

When he didn't answer, she said, "I imagine it is because you can help him."

Donna's husband got himself mired in the muck of his cases. She was used to this but didn't like it. In warmer weather, they rode bicycles together on the dirt backroads around Montpelier. Sam always found the ruts where he had to work twice as hard to churn the fat tires of his mountain bike through the mud, cursing. Donna did not sympathize with this miring part of the man. Ride over here where it's hard and dry, she thought but did not say.

"I suppose I can help him," said Sam. "I'm not even sure I want to, though. It's a pretty vile thing he wrote. On the other hand . . ." And he paused for a long moment. "On the other hand, it is a matter of free speech. That is the sacred principle. You know, people shouldn't be forbidden from speaking their minds, even if what they have to say is wrong. Even if it's hateful. Even if it's sacrilegious or flouts all convention. Uninhibited and robust speech—that's the language the Supreme Court once used. It's the price of democracy. Or maybe I should say the pride of democracy."

Donna was familiar with the plaque that hung behind Sam's desk in his office. It bore an inscription by Justice Louis Brandeis, the great progressive lawyer and jurist: *Those who won our independence believed that freedom to think as you will and to speak as you think are means indispensable to the discovery and spread of political truth.* It was a gift from a judge Sam had clerked for.

Next to the plaque were two framed charcoal drawings by Käthe Kollwitz, one a mother and her two hungry children, all with looks of despair, and the other a self-portrait of the artist hunched forward and gazing out into the world, also with despair. Donna's grandmother had purchased the drawings in 1936 from a gallery in her home town of Brno. Donna's mother had inherited them, and in turn they passed to Donna when her mother died in 1991.

They hung now in Sam's office because they suited his depressive mood more than Donna's. He loved them. She looked toward the wall across from the bed, where a cheerful watercolor of a sunflower painted by the Maine artist Harry Beskind warmed her heart, even now when she couldn't see it in the darkness.

"Okay, my sweet," she said. "I understand the point. So why the hesitation?"

"We might lose," Sam said. "Schools have some leeway to punish student speech when it crosses the line, if it really intrudes on the rights of other students. They're not quite full citizens in that respect." He removed his hand from Donna's bottom and ran his fingers up her spine. "God, Donna, what if I lose this case *and* Lucy Cross's appeal? Both! That's probably what'll happen. I have a sinking feeling."

"But Sam, you've been through these ups and downs before. It's part of being a lawyer, isn't it? I think you've told me that." Get out of the mud, Sam.

"Maybe. But this time I'm more invested in these cases. And it's not just the fear of losing," he said as he shifted his body in the bed. "Like I said, I'm having trouble defending what Ricky did. It was so bigoted. You heard what Sarah said when she was here at Thanksgiving." He stopped speaking, and she waited. "But who am I to judge? It's not up to me to set the boundaries of permissible speech. Fuck."

"Is that a command?" she asked.

"What?" Then he smiled, and Donna touched his face with her fingers. She traced the ridge of his brow, the notch between brow and nose, and the curve of his nose over to the soft upper lip. Sam spoke again after a moment. "So Sarah and I talked on the phone yesterday."

His relationship with his daughter was defined by a fractious quality. Donna could see that Sarah was often impatient with Sam and punctured his ideals with her pointed half-truths.

"She said I was crazy to take Ricky's case. She thinks I'm betraying the values I should be standing up for."

"When did you talk to her? Where was I?" A touch of jealousy here.

"Um, I think it was before you got home last night. You stopped for groceries at the Co-op. Remember, you brought home those fingerling potatoes? She called about 6:30. And you bought those spinach tortellini. And you forgot the ice cream."

"I didn't forget the ice cream. We don't need more ice cream. And you didn't tell me last night?"

"About the ice cream? What didn't I tell you?"

"No, idiot, about Sarah's call. You didn't tell me."

"Donna, come on. I guess I forgot. But that's not the point here."

"I like to know when she calls, you know that. But never

mind. I'm sorry, I just miss her. And *your* mind's on ice cream. Anyway, I think Sarah will understand. You have a client and you do what's right for him. No?"

"I'm not sure. She may be right. Ricky didn't have to become my client. That was my choice." He paused. "I know you miss her, Donna. Me too."

Sarah, like most Montpelier kids, was not coming back to live in her hometown. "We really wouldn't want her living at home, though," he added. "Would we? A little closer would be good. Or maybe more regular visits."

"Yeah," she sighed. "I miss having her around. We cooked together, we talked, we watched TV, even bad TV, we knitted together. You'd think I'd adjust. It's been quite a few years."

"You and I do all those things together, except for the knitting," said Sam. "We watch bad TV."

"I know, but not so often. And you're busy and ruminating on your cases. And you're not the same person as Sarah. You're male, for one."

"Very much," he said, and was quiet. Sam came back to his present worries. "You know, the poor kid is suffering. I mean Ricky. He's wracked with guilt. He told me he didn't want to hurt Kerry. He just feels she was a sinner and this thing needed to be public. A sinner! What was his expression? He said he thought Kerry needed to be brought into the light. Or maybe he wanted to bring light to her. Right. If anyone needs enlightening, it's Ricky."

Donna took her time, trying to figure out what troubled her. "If it was all private, a secret, how did he even know about her being gay?"

"That's an interesting part of this, Donna. She *told* him. These two kids were actually close, close enough that she had confided in him at some point. How's that for irony? Ricky says she was one of the only kids at school that *he could trust*. You know how socially isolated he is. And she must have felt the same way."

"Her trust was misplaced, I suppose." In the darkness Donna considered her next words. "Does Ricky feel he is responsible for her death?"

"Yeah, he seems to. But he wasn't responsible. You know the message he sent her on Facebook? He wrote that her being gay was a sin and whatnot and that maybe she should be outed so the world would know. Well, he never did follow through. He never actually posted this stuff or made it public."

"Do you know why? What happened?" Donna was propped up on an elbow.

"I think so. At any rate, this is what Ricky told me. Kerry phoned him after the Facebook message and left him a voice mail. Her message wasn't intelligible. She was totally distraught and crying. Ricky was all confused. So he thought maybe they should meet and talk about it face to face. He was having second thoughts. He was, I think, really upset by how Kerry reacted. Can you imagine?"

Sam stopped talking, pulled Donna toward him and kissed her. She responded for a moment, but stopped him, wanting to hear more.

"Like I said," he went on, "he really cared about Kerry. That's the irony again. That's why he sent her a second message, saying they should meet after school at the café, at Sacred Grounds."

"Did they meet?"

"Yes. She came. It was the next day. They really talked, for a long time. Ricky says he told her he wouldn't post the stuff about her being a lesbian. I'm not sure he ever would have in the first place, but after that phone call and their talk, definitely not. Seeing her so upset, I guess he had a change of heart. He was pretty emotional about it himself."

"Oh, that's good to hear. It confirms my feelings about Ricky, you know? So, Sam. How can he be responsible? Do you think he's telling the truth?"

"Ricky's honest as they come, even if he's wrongheaded. Yeah, I think he's telling the truth. He's not responsible for what Kerry did. But he thinks he is, Donna. Maybe she didn't believe him."

"And she took her life because she misunderstood? That poor girl. It's so horribly tragic."

"You know," he said after another few seconds, "I said Ricky's honest. But I feel like he's not telling me everything. I sense it. I tried to get more, but he got rigid and clammed up tight. His damned principles."

Sam was quiet and she had no more questions. She rolled back up against him. She loved his principles. Beneath the down comforter, she put her hand between his legs. "Now it's you becoming rigid in your advanced middle age," she said sweetly.

B arb Laval and Alicia Santana lay awake in another bed in their white clapboard farmhouse with the big side porch a few miles from downtown Montpelier, on the dirt road known locally as Bull Riley but which appeared on maps as Town Road 15. The road had a notorious washboard surface where it rose steeply from the Scape River valley. The house was perched close to the road, with an old barn immediately opposite. The barn was owned by the neighboring dairy farmer, who used it for tractor and equipment storage since he had put in a modern barn and milking parlor farther up the hill.

Many years before, the dairy farmer had painted TAKE BACK VERMONT in large white block letters across the red barn boards. The message was legible a quarter mile away, an early version of Facebook.

TAKE BACK VERMONT was the slogan used at that time to express the feelings of many Vermonters opposed to civil unions between same-sex partners, well before the era of same-sex marriage. When the realtor first showed Barb and Alicia the house on Bull Riley Road, they stood on the gravel drive with their backs to the house and studied the barn. They swallowed their pride, took the long view, and bought the house.

Soon after the move, they visited with the farmer and his wife, brought a pie baked with apples from the trees next to the old house, and helped him once during that first winter when his truck got stuck in a snowdrift in the barnyard. Alicia was generous with her smile. The dairy farmer repainted the barn in the early summer. Bright barn-red, no white letters. Message deleted.

In semi-darkness now, Barb turned toward Alicia. "I have a sense of loyalty to my school, Alicia. I know Gayle Peters can be hard. It's not about her. It's about the school." She said "aboat" like a Canadian.

Alicia was defensive. "It's not my case, Barb. It's Sam's. Ricky's his client."

Barb parried. "Sure, but you're his law partner and you're working on the case too. You said you've been doing the research, helping him prepare."

She was right. "Yes, okay, Barb. I am. We believe in it. I believe in it. Ricky Stillwell shouldn't have been expelled from school for spewing his religious ideas. He can't even walk in his own graduation. It's bad enough for him to suffer from the whole community turning on him. And his own conscience is killing him."

"Jesus, Alicia. Ricky is not the victim. And this isn't about religion, is it? It's homophobia. The school has to take a strong stand on that. You understand that as well as anyone." She looked sadly into her wife's dark eyes, barely visible in the moonlight. "Come on, Alicia. We've been there."

She was not Rosa Parks or Harvey Milk. But Barb was out there every day, visible in the front office, secretary to the principal, known well in the high school, a lesbian, sometimes admired, sometimes derided by the mean or ignorant. Whether she wished it or not, she stood as a role model for gay and lesbian students.

She had appeared in public with Alicia, and held hands with Alicia, at any number of school events. Truth be told, it was more Alicia's doing. But Barb assented.

They were not oblivious to the attention and gossip they drew. But if others could publicly display their affection to their spouses and girlfriends and boyfriends, as they often did, then surely so could Barb, in modest and proper fashion. And so she did. Here at a varsity basketball game, there at a school jazz concert, there again at *Guys and Dolls*, the school drama club's production three years before. Even at last year's graduation ceremony.

"Remember that poster a few years ago, Alicia? That awful thing the kids put on the bulletin board?"

"I remember," said Alicia.

Someone had posted copies of a flyer on school bulletin boards featuring a Xeroxed photograph of Barb Laval's head pasted to an image of a nude woman with large breasts. Below the collage, the anonymous artist had written, *Looking to get a head? Cum and see Miss Laval. Girls and boys are welcome.* "I think I was the only one who wasn't offended or outraged," Alicia said. "But I know it hurt you, Barb."

"It hurt, but I got support from a lot of students." For a week after the incident, the student LGBTSA—Lesbian Gay Bisexual Transgender Straight Alliance—maintained a silent vigil outside Barb's office, to her acute embarrassment and pleasure. "And Gayle was supportive too."

"Really? I don't remember that."

"She made sure to check in on me, several times. She did care, Alicia. And she also supported the LGB students who were demonstrating in the hallway. That was a big deal, and I think she took flak from some parents."

"Well, good." Alicia got up and went to the bathroom, and Barb didn't know what to make of her tone.

Returning to their bed, Alicia said, "I'm sorry, Barb, that sounded sarcastic, but I didn't mean it that way. It's good to hear Gayle Peters stuck with you. I guess I didn't realize it. What about her? Do you think she's queer?"

"I've wondered about it sometimes, but I really don't care. I never asked her or talked to her about it. Gayle's a mystery woman and keeps things very private. As far as I know, she's always been single."

"Still kind of strange," mused Alicia. "They never figured out who did it? The poster?"

"No. No one confessed, and no one ratted. We got over it and moved on." Barb now pulled Alicia toward her and whispered, "Kerry Pearson was just a beautiful person."

"Of course she was." Alicia could feel Barb's warm breath on her face.

"Tell me, Alicia. Explain it to me. How precious is speech that causes such deep pain? How free should it be?" Then holding her head back and looking directly at Alicia, she said, "And her mom Francine is one of your oldest friends, Alicia. Are you betraying her by defending Ricky?" But immediately she regretted saying it.

Alicia turned to the ceiling. "Betrayal is a terrible word." She pulled the flannel sheet tighter around her shoulders and thought about Fran and Kerry, and tears pressed into her eyes.

An image came to her mind of a dimpled three-year-old Kerry, cuddling next to her in a sunny law school classroom, as they played and drew pictures, while a professor taught about the law of search and seizure. That girl was so sweet and so perceptive! Fran had lost her only child, her perfect child, to suicide. It was grotesque.

Had she lost her heart, taking this case?

Barb softened. "I'm sorry, Alicia. I wasn't fair." She held Alicia's hand in hers, and brought it to her mouth. "Oh dear."

"I'm trying," Alicia said, "to keep things in separate boxes. I loved that girl too, and her mother. I know you know that."

They heard the distant train whistle in the night air. "But this case is about law and principle. It's like this. If Ricky can be silenced for his views, so can I for mine, and you for yours." She tried to see Barb's face. "Like all of us, he deserves respect. His autonomy and dignity deserve respect. Right?"

"How about Kerry's autonomy and dignity?"

"Hers too. But you don't respect her by silencing Ricky."

"Alicia, but what if what he says tramples on her privacy? He threatens to out her?"

"Yeah, okay, that could be a problem. I think you're right. But really, Barb, he wasn't doing that, in the end. Maybe he told her he might do that, but then he told her he wouldn't. The case is built on what really happened, not on what might have happened in a different world."

"Is that what Sam thinks too?" asked Barb.

Alicia thought for a moment. "More or less. But to be honest, Barb, he's more on the fence than I am. He's posed the same kind of questions you're asking."

"Really?" said Barb. "So they're not such dumb questions."

"No one ever said anything about dumb," said Alicia.

"Truthfully?" Barb continued. "I'm happy to hear that Sam and I find the same questions interesting. I do like that guy. Gruffness and all. You and Sam, it's still all good with you two, working together and all, eh?"

"Oh, for sure. I can tease him dreadfully and it's all good."

"No, seriously, Alicia."

"All right," she said. "We probably complement each other. I learn a lot from him because of his experience. He is careful and makes me slow down. He learns from me too, from whatever I have to offer. But you mean like running the firm?

We have no problems reaching decisions about that kind of stuff. But, sure, our personalities are very different. He can be heavy, you know, not quite depressed, I guess, but discouraged. And, well, you know me. Bouncing off the ceiling."

"I do know you," said Barb. "You have a huge talent for getting along with different personalities. Me, for instance."

"Yuh-huh. Sweetheart."

In the following lull, Alicia reached to Barb and stroked her smooth face, her forehead, cheeks, the full lips. Her shoulders, her arms, her breasts. Soft tissue.

"You know me, Barb," said Alicia again. "I get all hyped up about the majesty of the law. But you asked about Frannie? Yeah, I am betraying her. There is nothing majestic about that." She turned and pressed her full body up against her lover. They went to sleep way too late.

In the yellow house on Baker Street, at a very late hour for visitors, Francine Loughlin answered the knock. "Come in, Barry, yes, of course."

"You haven't been answering the phone or returning messages," the policeman said. "So I didn't know if it was all right to stop by, especially at this hour. I drove by and saw the light on. I don't want to intrude, Fran, but I just thought, maybe, it would be okay to come here."

"I'm not sleeping. You're not intruding. It is okay for you to come here. In fact, Barry, I'm relieved to have the company. To have your company."

In the kitchen she poured him a glass of red wine, and then one for herself, and he followed her to the living room carrying the bottle and his glass. She beckoned for him to sit on the sofa, a solid mission-style piece, and she sat right beside him, pulling her feet up under her. She said, "Barry, I don't know how to do this. I don't know how to survive."

She was looking into her glass. "I miss my girl so terribly. You look at me and you might think I'm all right, because I can get dressed and brush my hair and talk to you and pour wine from a bottle. But I'm not all right. I'm falling. I've been falling since I heard. I don't know when I'll hit ground."

Barry LaPorte did not know what to say about this. He had lost his older brother in Vietnam, so many years ago. He had been despondent when his wife left him, not so many years ago. He had gone on. But losing a child? He did not have words to console her. So he had the wisdom not to speak.

They sat in quiet. He drank the wine. He looked at Fran, weary green eyes in her intelligent suffering face, round and lined, with lush hair the color of cooked sweet potato falling back over the sofa and her shoulders, and he loved her, and wanted her to love him, and he drank a second glass of wine she poured, and he worried about crossing the boundary between professional and personal, and about the unsavory contradictions that followed.

Or maybe there was no contradiction?

He took hold of her hand and studied it. She let him, and that gave him the confidence to speak. "I love you," he said. He looked directly into her eyes. "Can you accept that?" He almost choked getting these words out, and he quickly stammered, "Look, I can just leave if I'm bothering you," and he stood up suddenly.

Fran tugged at his sleeve, bringing him back heavily onto the sofa. She smiled for the first time in two months. "I can accept that, old Barry." She kept smiling at him, and his heart turned into gold.

"You can?"

"I can. I do. I love you too. I think."

"Well, don't think too hard," said Barry. "Just leave it like that. For me, I just want you to know that I am in love with you, have been for years, always will be. That's how it is, all right? I want you to know it. I don't even need it to be reciprocal."

"You can stop talking now," she said.

She led him up the narrow stairs and showed him the bathroom and her bedroom. She found a new toothbrush for him and offered it. When he was alone in the bathroom he saw on a hook on the back of the door her cream-colored bathrobe, and the domestic intimacy promised by the simple bathrobe shocked him and he shivered as he brushed his teeth. He dried his face on her bathrobe.

In the cabinet behind the mirror above the sink, he found the dental floss amidst her creams and lotions, and those things too, those feminine products, startled him. He was an invasive species.

He inhaled deeply and breathed out slowly. Then he decided he had better wash himself, but in this foreign feminine bathroom he did not know quite how to manage it efficiently, and he wasn't sure which towel he should use and whether he should put his clothes back on. From a shelf next to the bathtub he chose a towel that was too small. He dried himself badly and got dressed again.

It all took longer than it should have and he felt ridiculous and conspicuous as he finally emerged. But there stood Fran in a nightgown, smiling at him.

"Would you like to remove those clothes now?" she asked. "I don't have any pajamas to lend you, but I hope that won't trouble you."

"It's all right with me, Frannie. Are you sure?" She did not give a verbal response but she kissed him and unbuttoned his shirt. She stood with her head pressed against his chest so she could hear his heart beat. She said she could hear it. It calmed his anxiety.

"Thank you for being here, Mr. Barry, darling Barry. I'm sorry, I'm not sure how to behave right now."

"You? I'm the one acting all weird. Look, Frannie, I just

want to be with you. I want to hold you and cuddle you. Whatever way you want. Kerry's death didn't change this, you know."

She looked at him with puzzlement. "Kerry's death has changed every single thing for me. Every fiber. There was a time before, and there is this time now. I'm not sure if there is a time after."

"Yes, I know that, Frannie, I understand, or I think I do. I'm sorry, what I said didn't sound right. I'm talking about my feelings for you; they haven't changed. It is just now that I'm expressing them, for some reason that I can't fathom. Did you know I felt this way for a long time?"

"Yes, I think so. You always looked at me searchingly." The covers were pulled back on the bed. Moments later they sat side by side, fully undressed. "And truthfully, Barry? I have felt close to you too for a long time. I was afraid to speak up."

Barry was in a state of euphoric shock, and could not express himself appropriately, as he looked searchingly at her naked body. "Wow," he said. "I've never seen so many freckles."

"Oh?"

"It so happens I like freckles."

"I don't show them to many people."

"Thank you," he said.

"Wow," he said, "you even have freckles down here."

"I didn't even know that myself. Are you sure?"

"Let me get a closer look," he said. "May I?"

The fact that Aaron's creation and transmission of the IM icon occurred away from school property does not necessarily insulate him from school discipline. . . . [I]t was reasonably foreseeable that

*the IM icon would come to the attention of school
authorities and the teacher whom the icon
depicted being shot.*

Wisniewski v. Board of Education of the Weedsport Central School District, 494 F.3d 34 (2d Cir. 2007)

Sam and Alicia met Clara and Ricky Stillwell in front of the Fred I. Parker Federal Courthouse in Burlington. It was a surprisingly warm morning for February, with bright sun, and no wind coming off Lake Champlain. Snow lay in clumps around the building. The building also housed the post office and other federal agencies. It was ugly, utilitarian and forbidding, features evident to Ricky and his mother as they stared at the lobby entrance.

"What do you think will happen today?" Ricky asked. They had talked about it already, but Ricky was nervous.

Sam studied his client. "Ricky, I can't be sure how it will go. I'd like to put our case on through Gayle Peters. We think her testimony should be enough to show they can't meet the *Tinker* test. I don't intend to have you testify today, but you might need to. I imagine the judge will want to hear legal argument too. That's her style. Remember, today is what we call a preliminary injunction hearing. Nothing final."

Courts scheduled these hearings promptly, as the point was to avoid continuing harm during the often long pendency of a case. Sometimes a court would preserve the status quo while a case ripened. If Ricky's claims had merit, then every day of the expulsion from school caused harm, and the school should be enjoined from imposing the expulsion until trial and judgment.

If the school had the better legal argument in the end, the court could, at that time, lift the injunction and permit the school to expel Ricky. As plaintiff, Ricky had the elusive burden at this stage of the case to show he was "likely to succeed on the merits" of his claim that the school district had violated his constitutional right of free speech. It was a trial run.

"So what do I do in there?" Ricky asked. "Just sit still and be quiet?"

"If you can do that, yup."

"I'm good at that," said Ricky. "At least the quiet part. I can't always sit still."

They wended through the court's security apparatus, installed in the wake of the Oklahoma City bombing two decades earlier, and took the elevator to the fifth floor courtroom. Already seated at the defendant's table near the judge's bench were Tad Sorowski, the school district's imposing counsel, wearing pin-stripes, and Superintendent Allen Bird at his side. Two members of the Montpelier school board hovered in the rear of the courtroom with the high school principal, Gayle Peters. Clara Stillwell, still a member of the school board, avoided eye contact, and took a seat in one of the pews.

Sam, Alicia and Ricky walked up the aisle and sat at the plaintiff's table, with Ricky sandwiched between the two lawyers. Sam sorted his papers and nodded to Sorowski and Allen.

"All rise," announced the courtroom bailiff, and in walked Judge Mildred Wallis. Sam knew Wallis from her days in private practice before her 1996 appointment to the bench. He had appeared before her recently, in the town meeting prayer case. She was nobody's fool. Early in her career, she had worked as counsel for the Senate Judiciary Committee, then chaired by Vermont's senior senator, Patrick Leahy. She was seriously overweight and appeared to be in pain.

"Please be seated. Good morning all. This is a preliminary injunction motion. I've reviewed your papers, though with less thoroughness than I would have liked. Before taking testimony,

I want to better understand your views on the off-campus speech problem."

She was referring to the fact that Stillwell's Facebook message was written during off-school hours, from an off-school location, on Stillwell's own computer. Limiting student speech in the school's classrooms and corridors during the school day was one thing. This was another. Limits on speech might be constitutionally permissible in the first case, but not the second. The law was built on distinctions. Facts and context were important. "Mr. Sorowski?"

Tad Sorowski stood, fastened one button of his suit jacket, as male lawyers enjoy doing when they stand in court, and was promptly interrupted by some commotion in the rear of the courtroom. Two young people, whom Ricky later confirmed were students at Montpelier High, stood up and held between them a large cloth, a sheet perhaps. As they stretched it taut, painted words were legible even to the judge at the front. The banner said:

HATES PEACH
LOVE FRUITS

Judge Wallis said, "Hates peach. Very cute, that."

The bailiff approached the bench and asked, "Shall I...?"

Judge Wallis shook her head. "No, if they remain quiet, let them be. Mr. Jacobson," she went on, "as the defender of unfettered speech in this litigation, you will not object, I assume?"

"That is correct, your Honor, I will not object."

"And Mr. Sorowski, if I read it right, these members of our gallery may be expressing a view in support of the school district's position, although, come to think of it, I am not so sure. Regardless, do you object if they stand mutely?"

"No, your Honor, I also will not object," said the barrister.

"But I assure you, I had no knowledge this was to occur, let alone did I approve such a demonstration."

"Of course not," the judge agreed.

"Not a very effective protest, if that's what it is," observed Sam Jacobson.

"But it's a fruitful one, surely," said the judge, twisting her mouth into something resembling a smile. She nodded for Sorowski to proceed.

Sorowski cleared his throat. "Your Honor. The case law of this Circuit"—he was speaking of the Second Circuit Court of Appeals, which comprises the federal districts of Vermont, New York and Connecticut—"is clear. In our opposition memorandum, I discussed the 2007 case entitled *Wisniewski v. Board of Education of the Weedsport Central School District.* The court there affirmed a judgment in favor of the school board."

Thanks to Alicia's research and preparation, Sam was familiar with *Wisniewski.* A middle school student, on his home computer, used a then-popular program called Instant Messenger or IM. He exchanged a series of messages with a group of his friends, some of whom were his school classmates. The messages themselves were perfectly innocuous.

The boy had, however, designed a personal icon to identify himself whenever he sent a message on the program. His icon was a small, crude drawing of a pistol firing a bullet at a person's head, with dots representing splattered blood. Beneath the drawing appeared the words "Kill Mr. VanderMolen." Mr. VanderMolen was a real person. He was the student's English teacher. Not so innocuous.

As it happens, a police investigator who interviewed the boy concluded that the icon was meant as a joke, and that he posed no real threat. A psychologist who evaluated him also found that he had no violent intent. Nevertheless, the school administration found that the icon was threatening and disruptive to school operations. The student was suspended for one semester and the teacher was allowed to stop teaching the class.

Sorowski summarized the facts for the judge, though he omitted what the police investigator and psychologist had found. "The court decided the case under the *Tinker* standard, your Honor, that it was reasonably foreseeable that Aaron Wisniewski's communication would cause a disruption within the school environment. That the communication was initiated from a computer in the boy's home did not endow the communication with enhanced protection under the First Amendment and therefore did not foreclose its regulation by school officials."

This was the manner in which Tad Sorowski spoke. He learned English only as a teenager, and perhaps that added formality to his diction. He was born in Poland, his father a Catholic poet of some renown after the war, who had miraculously survived two years in the Auschwitz extermination camp.

He went on. "The nexus with the school, your Honor, was deemed sufficient even though the student did not send any Instant Messages directly to the English teacher or to other school officials. Hence we have a direct parallel to the instant case. Mr. Stillwell did much the same thing, albeit using the Facebook program. Although the conduct of creating and distributing his messages occurred outside of school, it was in violation of school rules and disrupted school operations." Sorowski paused and looked up.

Judge Wallis asked, "Do you have more?"

"The Court of Appeals in the *Wisniewski* case therefore concluded, your Honor, that this student's computer messages were not protected by the First Amendment on the ground that there existed a reasonably foreseeable risk that the icon would come to the attention of school authorities and that it would materially and substantially disrupt the work and discipline of the school."

Clara Stillwell, sitting stiffly in the pew behind the plaintiff's counsel table, thought about this Wisniewski middle school boy. In his childish way, he had threatened to bring violence upon a teacher. Pictures of blood splattering from his English teacher's head! The boy was insolent and violent and deserved discipline. Her son was nothing like him. Ricky spoke truly from his religious beliefs, witnessing against sin.

How did the school's lawyer have the effrontery to compare the two? The Wisniewski boy was a hooligan. Her son, she thought, was a martyr. The Montpelier High School had a moral obligation to protect the rights of its religious students to speak and witness.

Ricky listened to Sorowski and felt sick with despair. His ruminations were nothing like his mother's. Aaron Wisniewski, he thought, was just a kid making a joke. He was playing a game with friends. The English teacher never got hurt.

But I, he thought, I wasn't playing a game. I meant what I wrote. I was serious. Kerry Pearson is dead. I am responsible. I could have acted. Done something, anything. I did nothing but sit on my useless hands.

He stared at his useless hands on the table before him and bowed his head until it banged the table. He used enough force to cause Judge Wallis to look worriedly at him. Alicia gently put her hand on his back.

Kowalski used the Internet to orchestrate a targeted attack on a classmate, and did so in a manner that was sufficiently connected to the school environment as to implicate the School District's recognized authority to discipline speech which "materially and substantially interfer[es] with the requirements of appropriate discipline in the

*operation of the school and collid[es] with
the rights of others."*

**Kowalski v. Berkeley County Schools,
652 F.3d 565, 567 (4th Cir. 2011)
(quoting [actually slightly misquoting]
Tinker v. Des Moines Independent Community
School District, 393 U.S. 503, 513 (1969))**

By this time, Alicia Santana had come to feel a surprising sympathy for Ricky Stillwell. She always had the capacity to love across boundaries, to love even those who hated her. She was feeling love now. It emanated from her, concentrated in the fingers of her left hand, in the middle of Ricky's back. Whatever offense arose from his Facebook message to Kerry, Alicia knew there was no malice in Ricky's intentions.

He had stumbled into a biblical bog of confusion and ignorance, and she did not want him to drown. Perhaps, she mused, she could help him find enlightenment. She left her hand in its place, her fingers spread between Ricky's shoulder blades. He let it stay.

When Alicia focused back on the proceedings, Tad Sorowski was discussing *Kowalski v. Berkeley County Schools*, a 2011 decision of the Fourth Circuit Court of Appeals based in Richmond, Virginia. Kowalski was a senior in high school who was suspended from school for creating an appalling webpage, on her home computer, using the social network program called MySpace. She gave her page an odd name, "Students Against Sluts Herpes," and it was filled with hateful mockery of another girl at the school. The creative juices of teenage sarcasm flowed in the wrong direction.

The court had, here too, found a sufficient connection to the school to justify applying the *Tinker* standard and to uphold the suspension. Sorowski made the obvious argument that Stillwell's conduct was similar in relevant respects to Kowalski's.

Judge Wallis stopped him here. "Mr. Jacobson or Ms. Santana? Who will argue for the plaintiff? Your turn."

Sam rose slowly to his feet, gathering focus. "First, Judge, the Supreme Court has never applied *Tinker* or other speech-limiting doctrines to student speech that occurs outside of school or school events. The First Amendment should have full sway in that context, and we should be cautious before applying lower court holdings that diminish the speaker's traditional freedom. Second, in the lower courts, the cases are not uniform. For example, we have the *en banc* Third Circuit issuing a decision in June 2011 called *Layshock v. Hermitage School District*."

He paused, making sure he had the judge's attention. "In *Layshock*, a high school student used his grandmother's computer during nonschool hours. His grandmother's computer—now that's a novelty."

The judge was not amused.

"The student created a fake MySpace profile of the school's principal. That is, this page was made to look as if it were the principal's own page on MySpace. This fake profile, Judge, had a lot of rude content. It contained obscenities and references to drug use. The student shared it with his friends and sooner or later, inevitably, it came to the attention of school authorities. The student was punished.

"It's just like *Kowalski* in that respect, Judge Wallis, a student using a computer outside of school to create an obscene MySpace page that circulated within the school population. The court—the *en banc* court, Judge"—Jacobson here making the point that the decision was made not by the usual panel of three appellate judges but by the entire panoply of Third Circuit judges—"held that the school district violated the student's First Amendment rights."

"I'm more interested in what goes on in the Second Circuit, Mr. Jacobson. How do you deal with *Wisniewski?*" She pronounced the name Wiz-new-ski.

Tad Sorowski had given the case's name what Sam assumed was the proper Polish pronunciation, something like Vish-nee-ef-ski. Who knew? The kid was American. Sorowski himself used an American pronunciation for his own name, the middle syllable given an accented long o sound, no hint of an ef.

Sam chose something in between and consequently mangled the name. "*Wisniewski* is distinguishable, Judge."

Distinguishing precedents was the favored gambit of legal argument. If a court ruled in favor of a school district in a prior case with apparently similar facts, the lawyer must show how the facts, despite appearances, are *not* similar in relevant respects to the pending case. Every law student learns the technique, and every appellate court applies it. And any number of legal scholars tries to show the project to be result-oriented gamesmanship.

"It's distinguishable for at least three reasons," Sam went on. "First, the case was about a violent message—a visual depiction of a gun and blood dripping from the English teacher's head. Or maybe the blood was even spurting. Morbidly violent. I think that's what really drives the case. So consider this just for a moment, Judge.

"Suppose a middle school student had sent an Instant Message to her buddies saying that she had a crush on her English teacher. A drawing of Mr. VanderMolen perhaps, surrounded by little hearts. I think we can agree it would be equally foreseeable that a message of that sort might come to the attention of classmates and school authorities and would cause just as much, or more, disruption to discipline at the school. Yet the law certainly would not or should not permit school authorities to suspend that hypothetical student from school for that hypothetical conduct. So *Wisniewski* really should be understood as limited to violent messages. And whatever we might say about Mr. Stillwell's message, he was not advocating violence."

He turned for a moment to look at his client, in the seat next to him, to establish just how nonviolent he was. Ricky complied.

"The second point is this," Jacobson continued. "There was a closer connection to the school in the *Wisniewski* case than there is here. The student had drawn and labeled a picture of his English teacher. His icon was directly related to the school. In contrast, Mr. Stillwell's message was written to his friend, his peer, who happened to be another student at the school. But there was nothing in his message that was inherently about the school. It was private.

"And that brings us to the third point, Judge. It was private. Unlike the other cases, this message never did get distributed to others; it never made it into the school. That's what the testimony would show. That is critical."

Sam stopped talking and looked at Judge Wallis, waiting to see if she had any questions for him. There were none. Tad Sorowski stood up to reply. Judge Wallis waved him back down. "No, I have enough on this issue, Mr. Sorowski. Thank you both for your cogent statements."

The judge was visibly uncomfortable. She stood up with effort. "It's a good time for lunch. Let's convene again at 1:30." Everyone stood on cue as she rose and maneuvered through the door behind the judge's bench.

May a public high school prohibit students from wearing T-shirts with messages that condemn and denigrate other students on the basis of their sexual orientation?

Harper v. Poway Unified School District, 445 F.3d 1166 (9th Cir. 2006), cert. granted; judgment vacated as moot, 549 U.S. 1262 (2007)

The bailiff called everyone back to attention as the judge stiffly resumed her place at the raised bench. The HATES PEACH banner-holders had retired and were seated.

"I've reviewed the cases," Judge Wallis said, getting right to the point. "Mr. Stillwell is a high school student. What he wrote on his computer was about another student at the same high school. It included a statement that he thought it might be beneficial to disclose his belief that she was a lesbian, as I understand it, and he specifically used the words 'the *whole* school will know.'" The judge paused to emphasize the point, raising her eyebrows into the wrinkles near her hairline.

"Therefore, without having heard the evidence, but based on your submissions, I conclude there appears to be a sufficient connection, in this case, between the Facebook message and the school to permit limitations on Mr. Stillwell's speech. This young man's speech act does not deserve the fullest protections of our First Amendment. The school may impose such limitations, but *only* if the school can satisfy the standard required by *Tinker*."

Judge Wallis paused again, looking at Jacobson. "And I do not subscribe to your view, Mr. Jacobson, that a school has authority only to regulate an explicitly violent message. There's nothing in the case law to support that conclusion. As to your argument that Mr. Stillwell's message was completely private and was never distributed to other students, well, let's hear what the evidence is. The message did make its way to Ms. Pearson, I take it—and perhaps with tragic consequences, though I certainly will not prejudge that point.

"At this stage, at least, the court rules that the defendant school district has cleared what we might call the *nexus* hurdle."

In other words, the speech could be treated, for First Amendment purposes, as if it had been made in school or on a school computer. The speaker could be punished if the *Tinker* test were met.

Alicia and Sam were prepared to lose this point. Indeed, they were eager to face *Tinker* head-on. Ricky's message should be protected under the mantle of the First Amendment because he was stating his viewpoint on a religious and social issue.

Alicia thought that Justice Sam Alito would rule in Ricky's favor, if one took seriously what he wrote in the *Bong Hits 4 Jesus* concurrence: the court would tolerate no restriction of student speech if the speech could be interpreted as commenting on a political or social issue.

Or, she feared, would the court overlook the substance of Ricky's *comment* and treat the communication as a *threat*? A true threat does not deserve First Amendment protection. Was it a true threat? It certainly wasn't a threat of violence.

In fact, if it were a threat, it was a threat to engage in more speech. But speech of a certain performative kind, she had to acknowledge; speech that invaded a person's privacy. "MAYBE YOU SHOULD BE OUTED AND THE WHOLE SCHOOL WILL KNOW." But then again, she mused, Ricky had written *should* not *will*. And he had written *Maybe*. What did Ricky mean? Did he intend to float an abstract moral proposition?— that in a righteous world, homosexuals would not be permitted to hide in the shadows?

Or did he mean to convey the concrete message—the threat—that he, Ricky Stillwell, was prepared, then and there, to disclose her aberrant sexual nature on Facebook? And if it were a threat, by the next day Ricky had *withdrawn* it. Does a withdrawn threat merit First Amendment protection?

Judge Wallis was now discussing *Harper v. Poway Unified School District. The Ninth Circuit Court of Appeals*, covering California and other western states, ruled against a student who was penalized for insisting on wearing a certain T-shirt to school. On the front of the shirt was written *Be ashamed, our school embraced what God has condemned*. On the back was the slogan *Homosexuality is shameful*.

It was the sort of T-shirt Ricky Stillwell might have worn. The school's need to protect its minority students from verbal assaults of this nature, the Ninth Circuit decided, trumped the free speech rights of the student with the T-shirt.

"I find Judge Reinhardt's opinion in *Harper*," intoned Judge Wallis, "to be persuasive." All the lawyers knew there was also a strong dissent filed by Chief Judge Alex Kozinski in *Harper*; this was a close issue that divided the Ninth Circuit. Judge Wallis was showing her hand. It was tipped toward the position of the Montpelier school board.

"But let's hear the evidence," she said. "I'd like you to focus on the *Tinker* issues—disruption of school programs and interference with other students' rights. Your burden of proof, Mr. Jacobson. Are you prepared to call a witness?"

Principal Gayle Peters came forward, swore to tell the truth, the whole truth, and nothing but the truth, and took her seat in the witness box. She was dressed in a charcoal suit and looked sharp, her dark hair with its white streak pulled back tight. Her lipstick was crimson. She looked over at Judge Wallis and then fixed her eyes on Sam. He was startled by the disdain in her face.

Calling the principal as his witness was a little unusual. Sam had chosen to present his case through the opposing party's representative. According to court protocol, he was permitted to treat her as a "hostile" witness and thus to pose the sort of leading and argumentative questions normally reserved for cross-examination.

They quickly established who she was and what she did and what her professional background was. And then Sam dived in, his trial lawyer persona overshadowing his usual phlegmatic character.

"In November of last year, the administration of the Montpelier School District decided to expel Ricky Stillwell from school, yes?"

"No."

She would not be an easy witness. "So tell me, what decision was made with respect to Ricky Stillwell last November?"

"We agreed that Ricky could work from home to complete his first semester courses and that he could graduate."

"But, Ms. Peters, the decision was made that he would not be allowed back in school from that date, through the end of the school year this June? Correct?"

"Yes."

"You don't want to call it an expulsion. Fine. And you recommended that decision?"

"It was not an expulsion. I along with others, the superintendent, Allen Bird, made this recommendation. And the school board adopted it. Mrs. Stillwell, one of the members of the school board, was asked to recuse herself. She did so."

"And you decided to do this based on the fact that Mr. Stillwell wrote a certain message on his own computer back in November, correct?"

"That's correct. Well, I'm not really certain whose computer it was."

"You knew it wasn't—you had no reason to think it was a school computer."

"That's true."

"And there was not any other reason for the expulsion, correct?"

"Expulsion?"

"There was no other reason for the action taken against Ricky, correct?"

"The decision was based on a particularly odious message he had sent to Kerry Pearson on Facebook. She was one of our high school seniors." Tragically *was*.

"Nothing else that Ricky did, in school or out of school, gave you reason to punish him?"

"No, it was because of the Facebook message."

Here he showed Peters an exhibit of the text of the Facebook message. "Yes," she said, when asked. "I believe that is an accurate copy."

"You agree with me that the message at issue was sent by Ricky only to Kerry Pearson, not to others?"

"I'm not certain of that."

"You have no evidence that it was sent to anyone other than Ms. Pearson, correct?"

She considered. "Yes, that's correct, at the time."

"What do you mean *at the time*? Do you have evidence the message was sent to people other than Ms. Pearson at some other time?"

"Yes. For example, I expect it was sent to the police when they investigated. A copy must have been sent to my office, because I saw it. I'm not sure who it came from now."

"All right, Ms. Peters. So let's be clear."

"I am being clear."

"Let's be clear," he repeated. On the table was a water pitcher and glasses. Sam poured and sipped. "Aside from the police and school administrators involved in the investigation of the incident, you have no evidence that Ricky Stillwell's Facebook message, the one in the exhibit, was sent to anyone other than Kerry Pearson, prior to the time that the school took action to punish him. Is that accurate, Ms. Peters?"

She reviewed the question in her mind, as she frowned briefly at the ceiling. "Correct."

"Or put it this way. No evidence that Ricky Stillwell, himself, sent or copied this message to anyone other than Ms. Pearson?"

Another pause and frown. "Again, not to my knowledge, Mr. Jacobson. But I do not really know what he did."

At some point during the principal's testimony, Ricky had closed his eyes, as if he could not bear to look at her.

"Your action, and the school board's action, in other words, were based only on the evidence you had, which was that Ricky Stillwell sent a message to just one individual?"

"We didn't know that."

"But, Ms. Peters, listen to the question. The school board's action was based on the evidence before it, can we agree on that?"

"Yes."

"And the evidence you had, again, was that Ricky Stillwell sent a message to just one individual, Kerry Pearson? You didn't have evidence that he sent it to anyone else. Correct?"

"Yes."

"And the message expressed his views about homosexuality and sin, correct?" In a moment Sam knew he made a mistake with this question; he had given her the room to amplify.

"The message, Mr. Jacobson, did more than express his hateful views about homosexuality and sin. It threatened to make Kerry's sexual orientation public."

"The message suggested Ricky Stillwell thought that maybe her sexual orientation *ought* to be made public, isn't that a more accurate way to say it, Ms. Peters? Here, let me show you the exhibit again."

"That may be your interpretation," she replied, as she glanced down at the exhibit. "I don't agree. He was threatening the girl. This was a terrible fear for her."

Sam paused and stared at her.

Peters had just testified that Kerry was afraid of having her sexual orientation become public knowledge. How did Peters know what Kerry feared or didn't fear?

Sam stood awkwardly at the counsel's table and struggled to find sense in this bit of testimony. Did the principal know, even before the Facebook incident, that Kerry Pearson was afraid of being outed? If so, did it mean she already knew that Kerry was gay? Unbelievably, Sam had not considered this possibility before, but the way Peters had answered the question suggested she did know. Acting on instinct, Sam asked, "Ms. Peters, you knew what Kerry's sexual orientation was before this incident came to light?"

She hesitated momentarily before answering. "Yes, I knew about that."

"And what was her sexual orientation?"

"Objection, your Honor," groaned Sorowski as he stood. "Relevance."

"Oh, come now," scolded Judge Wallis. "Of course it's relevant. Overruled."

"Please answer the question," said Jacobson.

"She was a lesbian," said the principal.

Tad Sorowski sat back down, his mouth clenched, trying to hide his bafflement. His rudder had been pulled out of the water. He too should have known this nugget of information. Gayle Peters had not told him. His mind raced to the implications. Did others at school, aside from the principal and Ricky Stillwell, already know about Kerry's sexual orientation? If it was already common knowledge, his theory was shot.

Sorowski had been proceeding under the theory that Stillwell's Facebook rant was so disturbing and destructive, and therefore not protected speech under the First Amendment, precisely because Stillwell had threatened to reveal something *private* about Kerry Pearson. Now, Sorowski wondered, had this girl's sexual orientation been so private after all? He would need to demonstrate to the court that it was, that the principal's knowledge of the fact was the exception. If, indeed, that were the case.

Sam, meanwhile, pondered his notes, looked over to Ricky, whose eyes were now open but offered no clue to what he was feeling, and back up to Gayle Peters, still defiant in the witness box. He was trying to figure this out. He stalled for time by repeating a question. "You knew she was a lesbian before you saw or heard about Mr. Stillwell's Facebook message?"

"Yes."

For the moment, Sam decided not to pursue the line, because he didn't know where it would lead, and he retreated to an earlier point. "To your knowledge, Mr. Stillwell did not send the Facebook message about Kerry Pearson, the one we have been discussing, to anyone at school other than Kerry herself, before the time when the administration decided to take action against Mr. Stillwell, is that correct?"

"I already answered that."

"Please answer the question."

"Would you repeat it then?" she demanded with exasperation.

Attorney Jacobson looked to the court reporter and nodded. She leaned in to study the tape emerging from her machine, and read the lawyer's last question. This did not displease Sam; Peters's truculence only served his purpose to emphasize this point.

"As I said before, I think that's correct, yes."

"And you didn't know that Mr. Stillwell intended to follow through, did you?"

"Follow through?"

"Fair enough, I wasn't clear. Ms. Peters, did you know, one way or the other, whether Mr. Stillwell actually intended to disclose Kerry's sexual orientation, that is to say, to out her at school?"

"I know that his message on the Facebook page implied he was going to do that. So, yes, I assumed that's what he intended."

"You assumed. Okay. You do know that he proposed to meet with her the following day?"

She took a moment over the question. "I'm not sure. I saw that just now on the exhibit. I believe I remember seeing something like that in the copy of the Facebook messages we saw at the time. I don't know whether they did meet."

"Okay, you don't know whether they did meet. And so you don't know what they said to each other, if they did meet, and whether or not Mr. Stillwell's intentions may have changed as a result of the meeting, isn't that correct?"

Gayle Peters answered, "Correct."

At the same moment, Tad Sorowski rose and said, "Objection. This is a compound, confusing question and it calls for speculation."

Judge Wallis, getting impatient and uncomfortable, announced, "We'll let the answer stand. The witness didn't know for certain that Mr. Stillwell was going to follow through on a threat. And how could she? She's not clairvoyant. Are we almost done?"

"Almost done, your Honor. You never"—Sam turned back to Peters—"met with Ricky Stillwell, at any time, before taking action against him? I mean a meeting that pertained to this incident?"

"I never met with him about this incident before making my recommendation, correct."

"So, before making your recommendation, you never inquired of Mr. Stillwell whether he had met with Ms. Pearson at the Sacred Grounds Café, as he had asked her to do? Right? You never made that inquiry?"

"That's right." She spat at him, or so it felt to Sam.

"And you also never asked him whether he intended to carry out this business of outing Kerry Pearson?"

"I didn't speak with him, Mr. Jacobson."

"Thank you," and Sam sat down. Without reason to believe Ricky would follow through with the threat, if that's what it was, the principal could not have had a reasonable belief that school activities and discipline would be substantially disrupted. At least one prong of the *Tinker* test was not satisfied.

Having disposed of preliminaries, Tad Sorowski asked, "Ms. Peters, please, when you learned what Mr. Stillwell had written on the Facebook program to Kerry Pearson, were you concerned about its content?"

"Yes, of course. It was an extremely hurtful message."

"Were you concerned about the effects of Mr. Stillwell's Facebook message in the school?"

"Absolutely concerned. A message calling homosexuality a sin, and threatening to disclose another student's sexual orientation, that sort of thing would tremendously disrupt what goes on in school. People would be talking about nothing else; students wouldn't be focused on the curriculum." Gayle Peters had been well prepped on these points.

A vibration of the table at which they sat caused Alicia to turn towards Ricky at her left. He was trembling and his eyes once again were closed.

"And were you concerned about the effects of the Facebook on Kerry Pearson?" Sorowski continued.

"Very much so. Ricky Stillwell's message would completely interfere with her rights as a student to have a safe environment at school." Again, more or less tracking *Tinker*.

Tad Sorowski took a step into a delicate area. "Why did you believe his message would have such an effect on Ms. Pearson?" he asked, looking intently at his witness.

"Why did I think so?"

"Yes, please."

"I knew this because there remains significant antagonism toward gay students at the high school. Some gay students have a very tough time."

"How did you know this message would specifically harm Kerry Pearson, Ms. Peters?"

"I knew Kerry Pearson. She was a senior and had been at the school all four years, and I was the principal all four years. I was also her lacrosse coach."

"And I think you told Mr. Jacobson, when he put questions to you a few moments ago, that you knew, in fact, that Ms. Pearson was a lesbian even before you learned of Mr. Stillwell's Facebook message?"

Gayle Peters shifted noticeably in her seat. "Yes, I knew."

Judge Wallis swiveled her chair to look directly at the witness in the box.

"How did you come upon this knowledge, Ms. Peters?"

"We had spoken about it. Kerry and I had spoken about it."

"When did that conversation occur?"

"Not just one conversation. There were many conversations. I can't say when exactly."

"Please tell us, as best as you can recall, when you and Kerry Pearson first had a conversation about her sexual orientation."

Gayle Peters was losing composure. She glanced around the courtroom. Clara Stillwell was leaning forward in her pew, her back rigid, staring at her.

Judge Wallis instructed the witness to please answer the question.

"I don't recall exactly. I think during Kerry's sophomore year."

Tad Sorowski did not want to reveal his surprise. A trial lawyer should never be in this predicament. He moved on gallantly. "You learned about Kerry's sexual orientation two years ago. All right. And did you speak with her about this subject on other occasions?"

"Yes, as I said, there were several conversations."

"Ms. Peters, are you aware if there were others at the school who also knew that Kerry was a lesbian?"

"Objection," interjected Sam. "Lack of foundation."

Judge Wallis pondered for a few seconds. "As the question is simply *Are you aware*, I believe your objection is premature. But assuming the witness does have some awareness of the situation, I'll allow her to elaborate. You can always examine the witness further, Mr. Jacobson. Overruled."

"Ms. Peters, do you have my question still in mind?" asked Sorowski.

"Yes."

"And your answer?"

"Yes, I am aware, and no, I don't think very many people at all knew about this subject. But it appears that Ricky Stillwell knew." Gayle's voice was hoarse.

Tad Sorowski let his breath out. Her answer was what he wanted to hear. But he had to show that the witness had a basis, a foundation, for her belief.

"Why do you believe that not many people knew about the subject, Ms. Peters?"

"She was a very private person when it came to this subject. I think she confided in me especially. She didn't want to be public about it. She told me."

"Why did she confide in you?"

Gayle was silent for several beats, distraught, glaring at the lawyers who stared at her in return. Tad waited while the question hung in the air.

"I don't know why," she said.

"Please, Ms. Peters, you must have some idea why this girl would share her secrets with you, with you *especially*, I think you said."

Sam stood. "Objection, calls for speculation."

"Your Honor, I am not asking for the witness to speculate. I am asking for her to state what she believes to be the case, within her realm of personal knowledge."

"Overruled. Proceed."

"Why, Ms. Peters, did Kerry Pearson share her secret with you especially?"

"She could confide in me because I was the school principal and I could be empathetic. I understood her."

"You understood her. Please explain what you mean."

"I understood her, Mr. Sorowski. I am also a gay woman. I understood. We could talk."

Sam swiveled about in his chair and caught Clara Stillwell's eye. She was boiling.

Tad saw the finish line and sprinted. "So Kerry Pearson knew about your own sexual orientation?"

"Yes, yes. We talked about this. We talked a lot."

"And these conversations were private? You believe Kerry did not share the same information with others?"

"Definitely not. Not at school. Her mother knew. But she, Kerry, was very secretive."

Tad Sorowski was done. In his haste, he knocked his water glass over his notes as he took his seat, and when he sprung up to save his papers, his chair fell backwards and crashed down. Judge Wallis ignored the tumult, called for a ten-minute recess, and lumbered off the bench.

❧

Ten minutes turned into thirty, and the judge returned. "Are you all right, Mr. Sorowski? Not to worry, I've taken worse tumbles in my life." Whether she was speaking literally was not entirely clear.

She sat heavily with a sigh, and waved her hand to indicate for everyone to take seats.

"Again, we're here on a preliminary injunction request. I'm not going to take further evidence. I believe the record is sufficient for me to make a determination."

The judge collected her thoughts, glanced at her notes, and continued. "It is not disputed that Mr. Stillwell's Facebook message remained a private message to Ms. Pearson. What Mr. Stillwell's intentions were might be disputed. But whatever his intentions might have been, the evidence presented shows that his Facebook posting was delivered only to Ms. Pearson and received only by Ms. Pearson. Based on those facts, the school district cannot have reasonably foreseen substantial disruption to its programs." She looked around the court and locked eyes with a chastened Tad Sorowski.

"The school district is unable, therefore, to satisfy at least the first prong of the Supreme Court's *Tinker* standard. This is so, especially in light of the fact that the *content* of the message touched on social and political matters of some importance, the kind of speech that receives the greatest protection under the First Amendment. I have in mind the *Saxe* case from the Third Circuit." This time the judge caught Sam's eye and perhaps nodded slightly in acknowledgment.

She shifted painfully in her seat. "I am somewhat more troubled by *Tinker's* second prong, whether the speech at issue would significantly interfere with the rights of other students at school. But here again, the message never made it to the school community. It remained a private dialogue between two students, one that took place outside of school, as far as the evidence shows. In a sense, I'm coming back to the nexus question."

Wallis seemed to be still thinking it through.

"This is not to minimize the deleterious effects this message might have had on Ms. Pearson. There is evidence that Ms. Pearson did not want her sexual orientation to be generally known. That is hardly surprising. But there appears to be no evidence of what, if any, effects the Facebook message actually had on her."

Judge Wallis leaned back in her chair and found a spot on the ceiling that seemed to hold her interest. The courtroom was silent. "If, I say *if*, Mr. Stillwell had followed through with his apparent threat—or even if there were evidence that he *would* have followed through—and had made public disclosures about Ms. Pearson's private personal life, with repercussions in the school, that would be a different case."

Wallis sat upright and turned her gaze on Ricky. She could not remain in one position. "And in that different case, the school district might well have acted within its constitutional authority to penalize such conduct. But he did not follow through, again, as far as the evidence shows. And the evidence at this stage of the proceedings also shows that school administrators had no sound reason to conclude that he would do so."

The judge looked at Ricky for an uncomfortably long moment. Ricky met her gaze. "The school administrators," she went on, "never bothered to ask him what he planned to do. I still don't know."

"And," the judge continued, "if Mr. Stillwell had distributed his more general anti-homosexual message throughout the school, then, too, we'd have a different case. We'd have the *Harper* T-shirt case from the Ninth Circuit. I won't say how I might have ruled in that one. But we don't have that."

Alicia looked over at Sam and could not suppress her momentary grin. Beyond Sam, she saw Principal Gayle Peters at the defendant's table. Gayle, so defiant earlier in the proceeding, now looked ragged.

Judge Wallis continued her summary, reading this time from her notes on the bench. "The court concludes, therefore, based on this preliminary record, that the defendant school district has not shown that its punishment of Mr. Stillwell, for the message he privately posted on Facebook, satisfies the standard articulated by the Supreme Court in *Tinker*. The evidence before the court is accordingly sufficient to show that the plaintiff is likely to prevail on the merits of his First Amendment claim."

Looking at Sorowski, she added, "And it appears to me most unlikely that additional evidence would demonstrate otherwise."

There was a final point the judge needed to make. "In addition to likelihood of success, the plaintiff must show irreparable harm in order to obtain an injunction. The kind of harm Mr. Stillwell is exposed to each day of his exclusion from school, whether the school's principal wants to call it an expulsion or not"—she cast a sardonic glance at the defense table—"that kind of harm is considered irreparable and cannot be compensated adequately by monetary damages. Accordingly, the motion for preliminary injunction is granted. The school district is enjoined, for the time being, from continuing to impose any adverse consequences upon the plaintiff."

Ignoring courtroom protocol, Gayle Peters asked, more with resignation than disbelief, "So we have to let Ricky come back to school?"

The judge did not answer her, but Sorowski whispered, "Yes."

Judge Wallis was poised to stand, but she paused and spoke to Sam. "Mr. Jacobson, I will ask you to prepare an order for the court's consideration. Fair enough? It's been a long day. We're adjourned."

❧

It was dark outside and much colder when the hearing ended. Alicia suggested they go somewhere for a bite. Clara declined; she was in no mood and had to get home, but Ricky could go with Alicia and Sam, if he wished, and get a ride home with them. Galled by the principal's revelations, Clara seemed intent on her own dark thoughts. She left them outside the lobby of the courthouse.

But Alicia was ebullient, and Sam was as close as he ever got to ebullient. Over steaming bowls of phô at Thoms Vietnamese restaurant, they applauded Judge Wallis for her deft appreciation of First Amendment doctrine, and they applauded each other. And that piece of work, Gayle Peters!

Ricky listened and ate soup. Alicia, mid-sentence in her giddy account of the twists of Peters's testimony, suddenly noticed his downcast expression, and shut herself off. He was plainly not sharing in the joy.

"Ricky?" she asked. Ricky looked around at the tables on either side, dabbed his chin with a napkin, cleared his throat, wished he had been more sparing with the pepper sauce, and felt altogether embarrassed by his own drama.

"What happened today, well, I'm glad Judge Wallis ruled our way," he said. "You did a great job, Sam. You guys were both great. I'm really appreciative of all you have done."

A pregnant *but* hung in the air as a waiter stopped by the table to inquire how the soup was. Yes, the soup is excellent, thank you.

Ricky rearranged his long legs under the table. "Do we have to keep pushing this?" he inquired, his eyes on his soup bowl, his jaw working. "I guess I want to end the case."

Sam's chopsticks, loaded with rice noodles, were halfway to his mouth. Ricky's comment froze him in that vulnerable position. He just looked up and waited.

"Look, I'm not going back in the high school anyway for sure. I've got all the credits I need to graduate, you know that. And I'm definitely not interested in getting money out of this. Can we just drop the case now? Like, declare a victory and walk out?"

Sam chewed and swallowed and blew his nose in the paper napkin. He understood enough to know not to push his client. Ricky had won a legal victory but would accept the punishment because his conscience demanded it. He had the right to free speech and he also had the right to accept blame and to pay penance for odious speech.

"Yeah, Ricky, I suppose we can do that. For now, I'll draft the preliminary injunction order and get that filed. All right? Let's make sure it gets signed by Judge Wallis. Then give it more thought. If this is what you want, we should be able to dismiss the case. Tad will agree."

Alicia added: "We'll want to make sure the school clears the record of your expulsion in exchange for us dismissing and your agreement not to return to school, something like that, right?" Sam nodded.

"That sounds okay." Ricky said. "You see, I think I realize..." He paused and stammered, "I was wrong. I knew it when I sat down with Kerry in the café. I knew it even then. I am pretty fucked up."

For a second time that day, Alicia reached out her hand to touch Ricky, this time on the side of his face, and she leaned in and kissed him on the cheek. "No you're not. We all have growing pains."

"Growing pains? No, that's no excuse. I don't understand it, being gay, being attracted to someone of the same sex. Really, I don't. I'm sorry. And my church does not condone it. Well, it's more than that. The church is disgusted by the whole concept. They say it's an abomination. You know. But none of that matters."

"What matters, Ricky," said Alicia, "is that you are figuring it out and doing your best as you go along. I admire you for that."

"I'm not figuring it out, really. That's what I'm saying. I just know I was wrong to come down on Kerry. She sure didn't deserve my criticism." He stopped talking and spooned the last of the beefy broth into his mouth, then looked back up at Alicia. "I think you are really kind, Alicia."

It's true, thought Sam, she is very kind. And like Alicia, he admired Ricky for his integrity. He just wasn't sure how best to express either of these sentiments and so he watched in silent appreciation.

Then Ricky suddenly got up, said he was feeling sick, and rushed off to the rest room. He returned in a few minutes and told them he had thrown up.

"The soup, you think?" asked Sam.

"Well, yeah, but that wasn't the reason," he said. "Just sick of myself."

"An act of expulsion, right?" said Alicia, and her big smile helped restore his courage.

Some time later, as they drove east down the highway, Sam tugged at his missing beard and grappled with a niggling enigma. If Kerry Pearson had confided in Gayle Peters so many times *before*, as Peters had revealed, why did she not go to Peters for guidance *after* getting Ricky's Facebook message? Why didn't this girl look to Peters for help then, at a time when she was so distraught and needed wise advice more than ever before?

Alicia was in the passenger seat next to him and Ricky was in the back, both quiet, in silent contemplation, or perhaps asleep. The car's headlights pierced the darkness enveloping them. Sam listened to the snow tires humming on the road, and he puzzled over the fact that Kerry had avoided Gayle Peters's confidence when she most needed it. He broke the peace and warily put the question to Ricky.

Ricky stayed quiet for several moments in the back seat. Then he said, "Why? I can't tell you why, Sam." He looked out into the dark.

Which only made Sam wonder whether Ricky meant he didn't *know* why, or he wouldn't *say* why. But Sam let it drop and asked another question that had been bothering him. "Ricky. Why didn't Kerry believe you at the Sacred Grounds that day when you told her you would keep everything private?"

"I can't say," said Ricky in close to a whisper. Sam caught Alicia's glance. He grimaced and decided he would cut his tongue out.

Ricky spoke again. "I think she did believe me." And a few seconds later, "I thought she did believe me."

They sped past the farms along the Scape River north of Church Township, and rode on to Montpelier in silence. Sam was eager to be home with Donna.

Part III
Principal Boundaries

By late March, the longer days and the sun's heat encouraged the delicate tips of crocuses to push through the waning snow in protected corners of Montpelier and surroundings. The warmth in the breeze softened the personality of the community. Pedestrians slowed their pace and stopped at street corners to greet one another.

It was not like native Vermonters to express pleasure. So they bemoaned the condition of Montpelier's streets: "Frost heaves bad up to Turley Crescent. Every year, same thing. Nobody fixes 'em." Or the legislature's failures: "They're still at it at the Statehouse, solving nothing. Yup, they'll stay there so long as we pay 'em for it. Every year, same thing. Nobody fixes it." No matter, the miracle was that they stopped to talk at all.

The transplants, on the other hand—who themselves or whose parents had moved to Vermont from points south or elsewhere—were more accustomed to wearing their emotions on their sleeves. They slipped easily back into wide smiles and bear hugs, shucking the burden of Seasonal Affective Disorder that had gripped them just a month earlier. Even the gelato shop on Chamber Street was doing a sprightly business. Hazelnut, cardamom pear, lemon ginger. Trendy salted caramel.

Ritvo's, the vintage clothing store and documentary film shop below Jacobson & Santana, had moved; in came a store selling raw pet food and pet supplies, catering to the vibrant raw pet food community of central Vermont.

Over at the high school, Charlie Siljadzic, the chair of the Montpelier Board of School Directors, heavy in the gut and heavy with duty, stopped in the outer office, greeted Barb Laval with a diffident nod, asked "Is she in?" and put his head into the principal's office to find elegant Gayle Peters at her desk reviewing the next fiscal year budget figures.

He stepped in and closed her office door and cleared his throat. "Hello Gayle. I'm sorry to interrupt, and sorry to deliver this letter to you. I'm going to leave it with you, and I'll be off." He did so, and he was. He closed her door again behind him as he left, with another nod to Barb Laval. "Lovely scarf," he told her, prompting Barb to pull the turquoise wrap tighter about her neck.

Gayle read the letter. She was not surprised. The school board had met in executive session last week. They had obtained a transcript of her testimony in federal court. They could hardly criticize her for having expelled Ricky Stillwell and exposing the district to liability in court and embarrassment in the press; that was a group decision, and they, the board, had concurred. No, this was about professional boundaries. They said she had crossed them.

The letter explained her transgression. She had met repeatedly with a student to discuss the most personal, private matters. By itself this was perhaps acceptable for a principal, although concerns were expressed about her having met with the minor student alone, and not having involved her mother, or even the school's guidance staff. What was clearly not acceptable, said the letter, was discussing her *own* sexuality with the student. Oh no, that crossed the line.

The board "regretfully" decided not to renew her contract. Principal Gayle Peters would be out of a job on June 30th. She could, if she wished, request a hearing before the board and "present any evidence and objections" she wished them to consider. They would finalize their decision at the next board meeting, hearing or no. Siljadzic left her his best regards. She was done.

And she was undone. Alone in her office, she imagined for a fleeting moment that Kerry Pearson was present, hovering across from the desk, the face of that bright young woman alive with hope. The image faded and she felt great sorrow about Kerry's fate, and her own. She called out, "Barb? Come in for a minute, will you? Close the door. Please."

Barb Laval would not presume to draw any conclusions from the school board chair's brief visit. So she was surprised to see Gayle Peters looking so utterly bleak. Gayle had been running her hands through her hair, leaving her dark sheaves with the striking streak of silver in an uncharacteristic mess.

"Oh, Gayle! What has happened? You look positively ill. Can I get you something?"

Gayle frowned at her and shook her head. "Barb, we are a despised group." Barb didn't know quite what she meant, and stared at Gayle in puzzlement. "Us," said Gayle. "They fucking hate us." Gayle handed Siljadzic's letter to Barb, who sat down and read it through twice.

"Oh, Gayle," said Barb once more. Barb could not manufacture sympathy; it flowed from her like a natural spring. "Oh, Gayle."

"Barb, do you think I should talk to Alicia? She does discrimination cases, right? I mean, I know she was there with Jacobson representing Ricky Stillwell, but that's over. And she'll understand this, won't she?"

Barb felt chilled and tucked her arms inside her turquoise silk wrap. She could answer only one of the principal's questions. "Alicia does handle discrimination cases. But, what are you thinking?"

"I'm thinking I'm not rolling over, Barb."

❧

Donna and Sam took a vacation. They went to see their daughter Sarah in Providence. Cherry blossoms brought cheer to the gritty littered streets in her neighborhood. Sarah was unusually cheery too. She was completing a year-long project of collecting and writing oral histories of a number of Providence residents who had come from Central America and the Dominican Republic and had opened up to her to recount their migration stories.

The project had begun as a form of community service undertaken in lieu of a prison sentence, following Sarah's conviction for unlawful trespass. Sarah, along with six members of her affinity group, known as Tahrir Square, had been arrested and later tried for occupying a downtown park in protest of wealth inequality.

Sam had argued with her over the utility of the action. The friction left a sore spot on both of their egos. But Sam recognized that Sarah had created a worthwhile project as a result of the converted sentence.

They were in the kitchen eating crackers and hummus. Brown rice simmered, root vegetables roasted, and local greenhouse greens sautéed. Sam opened a bottle of pinot grigio. Donna needed this break more than Sam; she had been complaining about the stresses of her counseling work. She could let down her hair here in Providence, a world away, and she took a full glass of wine, and sat on the old sofa incongruously situated next to the kitchen stove. She tucked her feet under her, smiled at Sarah, and let them prepare the meal.

Sarah stirred the sauté. "On the subject of forced migration," she said to her parents, "sometimes I still read the *Argus* on-line. There was an article, last week I think, saying Principal Peters will be leaving her job? They wouldn't give reasons. Do you know what's going on?"

Donna said, "Dad does know something about that."

"Does it have to do with Ricky's lawsuit?" Sarah asked.

"Well, not directly," Sam said. "Keep this confidential, okay? Her contract wasn't renewed for next year. It's because she had all these private meetings with Kerry Pearson. At Ricky's hearing, she testified that they talked about being gay—she's gay too. The board thought it was unprofessional."

"No, really? All this rampant homosexuality in little Montpelier, Vermont? What a dangerous place."

"Less dangerous with you gone." Sam stuck his elbow in her ribs. "But you know, the school board overreacts, like it did with Ricky. It's becoming a pattern. Peters actually has a decent discrimination case. Alicia has agreed to represent her."

"Alicia? Isn't that a conflict of interest or something? You guys just sued the school."

"Sure, but representing Peters isn't a conflict. It's the school district on the other side in both cases. Anyway, Ricky's case is over. We got a preliminary ruling in our favor on the First Amendment. I'm sure I told you. Ricky didn't want to go forward after that, and we dismissed the remainder of the case."

"Huh," she said. She turned off the burner under the sauté, grabbed a block of pecorino and gently grated it over the top of the greens, then covered the pan.

"You probably think that's for the better, Sarah," said Sam. "And maybe it was. But Judge Wallis did accept our central argument, that the school can't punish student speech about a public issue unless there's been some real disruption to the school. Alicia gets the credit; she really developed the arguments."

"Dad's being modest," said Donna.

"I get that, Dad, but there was more to it, wasn't there. We talked about this when I was up last Thanksgiving. You're being really wishy-washy here. Because Ricky's thing on Facebook threatened to reveal the fact that Kerry was gay. That, of all things, is *not* a public issue. Can't the school stop that kind of stuff?"

"Maybe the school could discipline a student for doing that. Maybe. But remember, Ricky never sent it to anyone else. In fact, he told her he wasn't going to. He came around."

"He came around," she repeated. "But, like, too late for her, right?"

"Don't jump to conclusions," he told her.

"Why not, if the conclusion is obvious?" The tension was familiar and unpleasant to both of them, like the rice now beginning to stick to the bottom of the pot. "It's what Meg thinks too," she added.

"You can't know this, and neither can Meg," he said. "The world is not always neat and tidy." He really wanted to divert the conversation. "Anyhow, I think Ricky just wants to move on. Literally. He's done with high school and done with Montpelier. He doesn't even still believe those things about homosexuality. He changed. In the end, he felt terrible guilt about it all. So, he's been driving around the country in his parents' old camper. You remember that thing?"

She nodded.

"And he'll be in New York City in the fall at NYU. He told me, by the way—Donna, you'll be interested—that he left that church he was going to."

Donna, sipping wine, said, "That's marvelous. I'm so glad."

Donna, Sam knew, was agnostic about atheism. She believed the world has a spiritual dimension, which means something indefinably more, she believed, than homage to the awesome wonder of the universe and the miracles of life and love. The indefinable part bothered Sam, precisely for that reason. He would ask her, what is it beyond beauty and nature itself that you find to be spiritual?

And Donna would answer that she couldn't put it into words, she felt it in her skin, in her nostrils, something bigger than us, something transcendent, and something sacred. "There is more to it that we just don't understand, that we cannot understand. Your science," she would say, as if science belonged to him, "does not have all the answers. I prefer to see the world as spiritual."

And Sam would sputter about preferences being irrelevant. "Oh man. It's not a question of what you prefer. It's not whether you like Lindt more than Cadbury. It's about what is real."

"Well, now you're trivializing it, Sam."

"Okay, forget chocolate," he would have said, as this terrain was well trod. "I'm not making it trivial. You prefer Renoir to Kandinsky and Mozart to Meatloaf. That's a matter of preference. Belief in evolution over divine creation is not about preference. It's about objective truth. And whether the universe is supervised by God or whether it's infected by spirits is not a matter of preference."

"You can be so profane," she would answer.

At the same time, Donna had no tolerance for organized Christian church ritual and uttering praises to Jesus. Donna would squirm with discomfort in her seat next to Sam on those occasions that found them in church for a Christian wedding or funeral service. She was so eager to get out into the fresh air, and Sam was always eager to follow. On that they could agree.

"All that preaching about sin," she now said, referring to Ricky's former house of worship. "How can anyone live a joyful life with that?"

Sarah asked, "What was the name of that church again?"

"Fellowship Church of the Crucified Savior," Sam responded. "You know, they have a child care center at the church. Next to the church building, out in that lot on the west side of the high school. In front there's a sign with the name of the church and an image of Jesus crucified on the cross, right over the name Happy Ducklings Daycare. How about that?"

"Sweet juxtaposition. Okay, I've decided," said Sarah.

"When I have children, if I have children, that's where I'm sending them."

"Good, that means you're coming home. And having children." Her mother. "Both good things. Will you live with us, then?"

"No," Sarah replied. "I'll just send my children up for extended stays. They will romp and quack with the happy ducklings under the crucifixion."

"Live with us or not," Donna mused, avoiding the joke, "we are always a family. We are woven together, the three of us like twirling strands in a braid. And your children will weave right in. You understand?"

Donna had worn braids as a young woman when she met Sam in New Haven. Sam used to unbraid her hair at night and kiss the back of her neck, so tenderly she would turn to him and melt into his embrace.

But her braided family rarely joined in her sentimentality. "The arrangement could get prickly," Sam said.

"Ouch," said Sarah, moaning at her father's crucifixion joke. "So Ricky's just traveling around the country, you said? It's hard to believe their old van still runs."

"Yup, it runs well, apparently. I got an email from him a couple of days ago, from Birmingham, Alabama, where he was staying for a week. He was really moved by a visit to the 16th Street Baptist Church, the place where those four girls were bombed."

"That sounds interesting," said Sarah. "He's traveling on his own?"

"On his own," Sam repeated. "I guess that suits him at this point. He says, though, he's meeting people couch-surfing. He told me he'd been staying with a Colombian woman called Valentina who works as a public defender in Birmingham, and that she'd been teaching him about racism and the prison system."

"Astonishing," Sarah posited, "how a person can transform himself." She returned to the other thread. "Dad, how did the school discriminate against Peters?"

Sam reverted to his serious-lawyer voice, an octave lower. "So," using the word that began most of his expositions, "we think the school board is treating Peters differently because she's gay. That's the theory. Straight people—teachers, administrators, whoever—can talk to students about their relationships. Nobody blinks. No, that's an overstatement. They blink, they hem and they haw and they kvetch, but nobody gets punished. But when Peters did the same thing, she's shown the door. She's booted out. So that's why we say it's discrimination."

Sarah nodded. "Sounds plausible." But she was unenthusiastic. She thought that litigation was a poor route to salvation. She asked, "Is that why she wants Alicia to represent her, because she thinks a lesbian lawyer will be better for her case?"

Sam scratched his chin. "No, probably not that exactly. I mean, she knows Alicia and Barb are lesbians, of course, since Barb works for her. It's no secret. But no, I think it's because Alicia is the best lawyer around for employment discrimination. Or as good as any, anyway. You know, when she was first out of law school, Alicia clerked with Broder Cavendish Carle and Sivitz in Burlington. They were the preeminent civil rights shop in the state."

Sam knew the firm well. One of the partners, Carle, who later became a law professor at American University, had once represented the teachers' union and brought a number of grievances against the Montpelier School District when the District closed its middle school two decades before and laid off several teachers, all of whom were women.

Donna too had encountered the firm, as it happened. Another partner, Broder, had challenged Donna's own department for not providing the full spectrum of vocational services to recent immigrants in Vermont. Like most, that case settled, with the State of Vermont agreeing to expand the services. But not before Donna had been called as a deposition witness and, as she later complained to Sam, spent an uncomfortable couple of hours subjected to Broder's vigorous questioning.

But the firm had achieved fame for its role in another case. "Weren't they the lawyers," Sarah asked, "who brought the suit to challenge the state's marriage law? The case that led to civil unions?"

"That's right," said Sam. "Civil unions was the legislature's response to the Vermont Supreme Court ruling. Half an apple. That wasn't what the lawyers were asking for."

"Maybe half an apple," said Donna, "but I think they were dealing with political reality at the time and were worried about intense backlash. It might have been the smartest way to move forward."

"Probably true," said Sam. After a moment of consideration and another sip of the pinot, Sam added, "I don't like Principal Peters's case much myself."

"Really, Sam?" said Donna from the sofa.

"Legally, it's probably okay. It's a bit hard to explain." A suite of sirens outside interrupted his thoughts. "You know, taking Ricky's case was a challenge because what he wrote was awful. But we were defending the principle of free speech. And somehow just as important for me, I believe in Ricky, in his goodness. In the love in his heart. You've heard me say it before."

"Aw shucks," said Sarah.

"How is it that you are more cynical than me?" said Sam.

"Than I?" replied Sarah without a beat, a blow in their longstanding battle of grammatical correctness.

Sam ignored her. "With Gayle Peters, okay, there's a principle there too. Awful pun, not intended." Sarah pretended to retch, but Sam continued the thought. "Maybe she was treated unfavorably because of her being gay. But here's my point: I don't believe in *her.*"

Donna tilted her head and smiled at Sam. Here he was again, judging a person by the love in their heart, as he put it. But how do you know what's in the heart, other than by their actions in the world? Didn't he think Gayle Peters had love in her heart? Maybe her husband had a special sensory organ to detect such things. He, who so adamantly believed in science.

Donna drank a bit more wine, her glass almost empty now, and Sarah pulled the roasting vegetables out of the oven. Her mother saw, for the first time in this moment as Sarah slid the roasting pan from the oven rack, that her daughter had become a grown-up. Sarah had moved inconspicuously from one station in life to another and was now a peer—had been for some time, Donna surmised, but only noticed in this kitchen instant. It made her happy.

"So father," Sarah said, unconscious of her mother's revelation, as she picked out a parsnip chunk, blew hard on it, and tasted.

"Not bad. Mmmm. Needs rosemary, and a bit more time in the oven," and she sprinkled rosemary and more salt over the concoction and slid the pan back in and closed the oven door.

"So father. Vot duz ziss mean, to belieff in a client?" Her father's Talmudic diversions inspired her to try on an absurd German-Jewish accent. The wine helped.

"Oy. You should have seen her on the stand at Ricky's hearing," Sam went on. "Defiant, contemptuous, arrogant. At least Ricky's humble. I've come to admire humility over the years."

"I remember Peters started as principal when I was a junior. She taught special ed before that. I thought she was a good principal, back in the day."

"Back in the day?" said Donna. "I'm sorry, you're not eligible to use that expression. You need to be of a certain age."

"Like, she was really supportive of the composting project." Sarah had helped organize an effort to collect the school kitchen waste for distribution to the Montpelier community gardens, an acre of lots alongside Mahady Park. "Ms. Peters was into it. I mean not into the compost itself; she didn't want to get her hands dirty. But she liked us, the organizers, and encouraged us."

Sarah drank some wine. "She understood, which is more than I can say for most of the adults in the school at the time. They thought we were nuts."

Sarah brought the hot pot of rice to the center of the table, set it down on an oven mitt, and stuck a wooden spoon upright in the middle of it. "Is Peters still the lacrosse coach? The lacrosse girls used to love her. Meg Stillwell played on the team for a couple of years."

She and Sam were setting the table. "Now that I think back, there was some conflict with one of the team members. It was Amber McGillavrey, remember her? Or I suppose really it was with Amber's mom. She didn't get the playing time her mom thought she deserved. Blah, blah. Meg said Ms. Peters was fair."

"Anyway," said Sam, "it's Alicia's case. And Alicia seems to like her enough. But then Alicia's always upbeat. Upbeat to a fault."

"Oh Sam," said Donna. "No such thing. You, however, could use a little more upbeat." They sat down at the kitchen table.

"Since you brought up Meg," Sam went on, as food was dished onto plates, "sometimes I think Clara Stillwell, bless her heart, is on a crusade to Christianize the schools. For her, it's not just about Christmas music." Donna emptied the last of the pinot into the three glasses. "She'd like to purge the school of homosexuals. Purge Peters, too. And if she could, she'd have the teachers leading the kids in prayer every morning."

"God forbid," Sarah said. "Like that town up in northern Vermont where they pray at town meeting. Aren't you still working on that case? Clara should move there."

"Actually," said Sam, "you saying that reminds me that a number of folks up in Jefferson have told Lucy Cross—she's my client in the town meeting case—that *she* should move out of town. Serious. You don't want to be in their company."

"No, you're right, Dad, I don't. Bad joke."

"Excellent dinner," said Donna. "You've become a good cook."

"I learned how from you," Sarah said.

"Nothing from me?" asked Sam.

"Oh Dad," said Sarah, "I have learned plenty from you. But cooking? Mostly from Mom. Except for soups. I've learned soups from you."

"That's right," said Donna. "Soups and argument."

After dinner, they took a stroll in the neighborhood among the flowering cherries, and returned to the apartment to enjoy a bottle of Italian dessert wine while they watched a special on public TV about theocracy in Iran.

It shall be an unlawful employment practice...for any employer... to discriminate against any individual because of race, color, religion, ancestry, national origin, sex, sexual orientation, gender identity, place of birth, or age or against a qualified disabled individual."

Title 21, Vermont Statutes Annotated, § 495(a)(1)

In the second floor law office on Chamber Street, above the raw pet food shop (still in business), the window was open to the breezes and noises of the street. Lawyer Alicia Santana and school principal Gayle Peters were discussing the latest developments in their discrimination case against the school district. On the sidewalk below the conference room, they could hear dogs growling at each other, and their owners trying to mediate. The sausage guy was setting up his stand down the street. A couple of Harleys roared by, stopped at the Sproul Street traffic light, and revved their engines, just to be noticed and annoying, and Alicia closed the window and wished that Montpelier would pass an ordinance prohibiting unmuffled motorcycles downtown, all violators to be castrated. Castration, she mused, might cure a lot of the world's ills.

Before bringing suit, Alicia had begun a discussion with Tad Sorowski, the school board's lawyer. She shared an outline of her argument. Would the school board see wisdom and reverse its decision? No, they would not.

Well then, would they discuss a reasonable financial settlement before we raise the litigation ante? No, not that either. What is there to discuss, asked Sorowski, with the evidence of wrongdoing so clear? So suit was filed in state court.

They were in state court rather than federal court because their discrimination claim arose under state law rather than federal law. Federal law still allowed discrimination on the basis of sexual orientation. In large parts of the country, it was permissible to fire someone, or not to hire in the first place, because the person was gay. But not, thank God, in Vermont.

So the case would be heard before Vermont Judge Dennis Affonco, now sitting in the county superior court, with its handsome clock tower, across from the Sacred Grounds Café on Chamber Street in Montpelier.

The school district had filed a motion for summary judgment. Summary judgment may be issued by a judge in a case where no facts are in dispute, hence no reason for witnesses, testimony, or other evidence; in short, no reason for a trial.

As laid bare in Tad Sorowski's motion, and recapitulated by Alicia for Gayle, the school district proposed the following facts were undisputed: First, Principal Peters had an employment contract with the school district that would continue from year to year, unless the school board determined there was "just and sufficient cause" to terminate the contract. Second, Peters had spoken with a high school student on multiple occasions about both the student's and her own experiences in life as a lesbian. Third, the board had determined that these personal conversations fell beyond the boundaries of professional propriety.

Fair enough, those three facts were undisputed.

And those three facts were sufficient, Sorowski argued. Based on that undisputed record, the court must find "as a matter of law," he wrote in his motion, that the school district had the legal authority to terminate the principal's contract for just cause. There was no discrimination at play.

Not so fast. Principal Peters and her lawyer had other ideas. They would show that other professionals at the school, heterosexual professionals, had, without suffering serious adverse consequences to *their* jobs, talked with students about *their* relationships, their heterosexual relationships. The inference to be drawn was that Gayle Peters had lost her job only because of her sexual orientation.

Sure, the school board could fire an employee for cause. But it could not fire an employee because she is a lesbian. Not all reasons are lawful reasons. Not all causes are just causes.

Gayle had recalled several instances. "Like Danielle Shen," she told Alicia. "She's a physical education teacher and the field hockey coach. She seems to have perpetual boyfriend troubles and as far as I can tell, she shares all the details with the entire field hockey team."

"Good, good, good," said Alicia. "Were there any consequences?"

"Basically, no." There had been a notorious incident the previous year. One of a string of unpleasant boyfriends had stalked onto the sidelines of the field during a quarterfinal against Mount Abenaki. Girls with raised sticks heroically surrounded the brute and ushered him off to cacophonous applause of the Montpelier student fans and bewildered consternation of everyone else.

"Shen wasn't disciplined," Gayle went on. "As I recall, there was a discussion and maybe a letter admonishing her, but no discipline beyond that, let alone dismissal. Needless to say, Shen is a heterosexual."

"Okay," Alicia prompted, her leg vibrating beneath the table, "what else?"

Gayle told her about John Carruthers, physics teacher, ex-hippie, and Kerry Pearson's advisor. Everyone seemed to know of his recent marital problems, which had become the topic *du jour* among his advisory group. Carruthers had his wrist slapped, nothing more, for asking students during one morning meeting how they felt about multiple sexual partners, an approach to marriage his wife apparently favored. Though uncorroborated, one sophomore boy reported hearing Carruthers mutter that if he ever again caught his wife fucking another guy, he would apply electrodes to the john's balls. The student informant was deemed unreliable.

Carruthers, too, was a heterosexual.

Another case was more wholesome. Sandra Winchester used to bring her baby to her elective on human biology and development to add a dash of life experience, with a whiff of diaper, to the curriculum. Winchester had cleared the pioneering program in advance with Peters and Bird, though the class discussion strayed from the approved syllabus into the more intimate and controversial territory of the birthing experience itself and what had led to it. In short, Sandra Winchester talked to her students about heterosexual love and sex. This was embarrassing especially for the high school technology coordinator, a very shy man. He was her husband.

"Alicia, Sandra even breast-fed her baby in front of students. As you might expect, the girls handled this just fine. But the boys? Oh, not the boys. They got way over-excited and over-stimulated. We had to immediately curtail that unapproved part of the program."

Alicia asked if any discipline had been imposed on Sandra Winchester. "No, none whatsoever." Gayle said this with bitterness.

Alicia soaked up the stories, furiously taking notes. She admired Gayle's intelligence, her grasp of the relevant detail. "I like this, Gayle," she told her. "This is good. These teachers, Shen, Carruthers and Winchester, they open a window. They share their heterosexual adventures with their students. Who they're fucking. And what happens to them?"

"No serious repercussions to their careers," answered Peters. "And it's whom."

"Hoom?"

"Whom they're fucking. Or whom their wives are fucking, in Carruthers's case. Either way, the ones being fucked are direct objects."

"Objects of desire, as well as grammar," said Alicia. "Anyway, they breach the boundaries of professional decorum but with no serious repercussions, like you said. But with you, well, you're a lesbian, right? And you don't have the same liberty. You are treated differently. In fact, what you did here was pretty modest compared to the others."

"Modest?" asked Gayle.

"Well, you just talked with one student, right?"

"I talked with just one student." Gayle ran her hand through her hair, the silver shock spilling forward.

"Exactly," said Alicia. "One rather mature student, who was apparently not in the least upset by what she heard. To the contrary. You weren't treated the same, Gayle."

"So it's discrimination," Gayle agreed. "No, Kerry Pearson wasn't at all bothered by our discussions. More than that, she was the one who came to *me*—for *help*."

Alicia nodded and smiled at her client.

At this stage of the litigation, they needed to present the information in an appropriate format to Judge Affonco. Gayle Peters would submit an affidavit detailing what Alicia began to call "the straight facts." If they could survive summary judgment, they would later substantiate their assertions with additional evidence obtained in discovery—the term lawyers use for the formal process of gathering information held by the opposing party or by potential witnesses.

They would examine the personnel records of Carruthers, Shen, Winchester—and others too that Gayle suspected— and prove that straights were given a free pass when it came to sex talk that was never available to Principal Gayle Peters. The evidence would show, they believed, that the school's rationale for firing Peters, *unprofessionalism*, was truly a pretext for bias against gays and lesbians. Behind the pretextual façade lurked the real, underlying unlawful motivation to treat homosexuals with less favor than their hetero counterparts.

For Alicia, the suit was redemptive. She had taken some flak for defending Ricky Stillwell's right to voice his anti-gay opinions. This case, on the other hand, was morally straightforward. That's how she described the situation to Barb Laval while they walked from the Farmer's Market to the yoga studio on Saturday morning, ahead of the coming rain storm.

Alicia carried their purple yoga mats and Barb, wearing a cantaloupe-colored fleece that Alicia had told her was too warm for the weather, toted a canvas shopping bag, filled with snap peas, fennel, assorted greens, and a loaf of seeded baguette, all from the Farmer's Market, which occupied the big parking lot behind the Chamber Street courthouse on Saturday mornings, spring through fall.

Barb was not too certain. "You really think it's a good case? I mean, Gayle shouldn't have told Kerry Pearson about her own stuff."

They approached Sproul Street, and Alicia spied Sergeant Barry LaPorte in uniform on the far side, and waved. He's a trooper, she thought, for she had heard how he had moved in with Francine and was helping Francine to heal. That was the common view among Frannie's friends.

"No, Barb, it's a good case."

Alicia felt a touch defensive. This is so typical of Barb, she thought, as they rounded the corner, always wavering and doubtful. Alicia sometimes wanted to put a rod in her backbone.

"Gayle Peters is a terrific leader and she got screwed. The thing is, Barb, the school district doesn't fire straight folks when they talk with students about sex. You should hear some of the stories. Well, you probably know most of them better than I do."

She offered a wry smile to Barb. "But they fired Peters, really for supporting a female gay student who needed help. Don't you see? This is the old fear of queers rearing its head. Royally pisses me off."

"But Alicia, you defended Ricky Stillwell when he was doing just the opposite, eh?" Barb stopped on the sidewalk, perplexed by the irritation she felt bubbling inside her. She put the bag down on the sidewalk and tore the end off the seeded baguette. She put it in her mouth and chewed. "Sometimes I don't understand you very well. Nothing is sacred."

"There are different principles at work, Barb. One principle is freedom of speech. That's Ricky. The other is equality. That's Gayle. Everyone has the right to live and work and be a part of it all, without having to confront barriers based on sex or status. You know this."

Alicia fixed her black eyes on Barb and added: "The principles are connected, Barb, because both serve democracy in its deep-down sense. And both protect the dignity of the individual. It's like a unified theory in physics to account for all the elemental forces in the universe."

Alicia gently put her hands on Barb's shoulders. Gusts of wind picked up the winter's dust and grit from the street. "Right?" she concluded.

"Maybe," said Barb, returning her gaze. "Except the physicists, as far as I understand it, which is not very far, have failed in their attempt to describe a unified theory. The very large and the very small don't reconcile. Neither do freedom and equality."

Barb placed the canvas bag back on her shoulder, taking care not to damage the protruding fennel tops. The bag sported the logo of a local microbrew, The Alchemist's Heady Topper. It featured an image of a wild-looking man, who bore a passing resemblance to Sam Jacobson, with what might be a garden of hops sprouting from the top of his head.

"This is tough and knotty," said Barb. "That's what I think. Knotty with a k."

"I agree with you about that, Barb. Knotty with a k. And Barb," Alicia said, "listen, I love you."

"You're changing the subject, Alicia," but she said this with a smile. "Why would you? Love me, that is."

"Love you? That's also one of the elemental forces of the universe. And because, Barb, you are the soul of goodness. That's why I love you. Plus your Canadian accent, eh? Plus your buns are beautiful." All of which was true.

Alicia held the door for Barb and admired her beautiful Canadian buns as they climbed the steep stairs to the yoga studio, Downward Dog, with vegetables, baguette, and yoga mats in hand, leaving their irritation with the grit on the street below.

⚒

Judge Dennis Affonco came to Albany, New York, as a young refugee from Cambodia. He entered college and then law school in Albany, later moving to Thetford, Vermont, when he fell in love and married a fourth-generation Vermont dairy farmer, who now raised and milked goats instead of cows. They made goat cheese.

He also built a respected legal practice in neighboring Norwich, and was appointed judge by then-governor of Vermont Howard Dean, who generally disliked lawyers but appointed some good judges nonetheless. Judge Affonco wore a bow tie and was slow to reach decisions. He was still married to the goat farmer and every year was re-elected as the moderator at the Thetford town meeting. They did not pray publicly in Thetford, except at church, and annually on August 6 to commemorate the atomic bombing of Hiroshima.

Judge Affonco called the lawyers to court to hear arguments on the summary judgment motion in *Peters v. Board of Directors of the Montpelier School District*. As expected, Tad Sorowski emphasized the school's authority as employer and the "egregious improprieties" committed by Principal Gayle Peters.

Principal Peters sat at the plaintiff's table a few feet away, stoically and miserably listening to the lawyer deliver his brief with his customary pedantry.

Sam Jacobson was present, as a curious observer, watching the proceedings from the rear of the courtroom. After his experience cross-examining Gayle Peters in Ricky's federal case, he kept a distance from her, hoping any bad blood between them did not infect her relationship with Alicia. He also retained a fixed interest in the woman.

He had had a dream about her, a rehash of the testimony during Ricky's hearing. From the witness box she attacked him ferociously, her fingernails bloody red as she lashed at him. In the dream he struggled with an exhibit. The exhibit would have explained everything, and he wanted to show it to Judge Wallis, but somehow he couldn't pull it out of an envelope, as if it were glued inside, and Peters laughed at him.

It would have made everything clear. But the exhibit wouldn't be revealed, even to himself. Sam did not understand, and he cursed the dullness of his mossy mind.

Sorowski finished and sat down, without causing any mayhem with the water pitcher or his chair, and Alicia Santana stood to argue. She stated in turn that her client's affidavit established sufficient evidence of pretext. "We have to have the opportunity to develop these facts in discovery and at trial, Judge."

Judge Affonco was doubtful. "How are any of these people mentioned in the affidavit similarly situated to the school's principal? A physics teacher, a gym teacher, a—what, biology teacher? None are senior administrators. None have the same level of responsibility. Is the school not permitted to make that distinction, to have a higher standard of professionalism, as it were, for a higher professional?"

"They can argue that, Judge. But it's a question for the jury. We have enough evidence to make out a *prima facie* case of discrimination, and enough evidence to persuade a jury that the school district's asserted rationale, though neutral on its face, in fact is a pretext cloaking invidious bias against gays and lesbians."

Tad Sorowski stood and was recognized by the judge. "What the plaintiff seeks to do, your Honor, is to pore through the private and confidential personnel files of these teachers."

Alicia popped up. "Personnel files that the plaintiff, who is the school principal, remember, has full access to in any event. We don't even need permission to view them."

"With respect, your Honor, I doubt that the principal, in her current incarnation as the plaintiff suing the school, has such access. In any event, however, this misses the point I was preparing to make. The issue is not so much access to the confidential personnel files. The issue is the use of evidence from the files in a public court proceeding."

Judge Affonco held up both hands. "All right. Not going to give you summary judgment at this time, Mr. Sorowski. Not to say I think this case will ever get to a jury. Plaintiff must come forward with evidence from which a jury can legitimately infer discriminatory animus on the school board's part. The court is doubtful on this score.

"The accumulation of material from the personnel files of teachers at the school will not necessarily meet the plaintiff's burden. Nevertheless, the motion is premature. Discovery should proceed. But limits are appropriate."

The judge bobbed his head at Sorowski and Santana in turn. "Why don't you counselors agree on a protective order governing how the personnel files will be treated." It was not a question.

He instructed the defendant next. "Mr. Sorowski, your client should produce copies of the requested files to Ms. Santana, on the condition that Ms. Santana and her client maintain the confidentiality of the files. If you locate documents, Ms. Santana, that you believe have evidentiary value in this case, then they can be submitted under seal to the court for review. Something along those lines. All right?"

"Thank you, Judge," said Alicia, rising. "That would be acceptable to the plaintiff. There is an additional point I'd like permission to raise, Judge." Alicia waited for a signal to go forward.

Affonco nodded.

"We requested that the school board produce copies of all communications to and among school board members that have any bearing on the decision to terminate Ms. Peters's contract. Plainly we have a right to those communications."

"Yes, that's fair. What is the problem?"

"What was produced, it appears to me, are only communications that included the board's chairman, Mr. Siljadzic." She spelled the name for the benefit of the court reporter. "These are emails, Judge. What we received were emails evidently downloaded and printed from Mr. Siljadzic's computer. You can see that from the header on the emails. He was either the sender or a recipient of the emails. Sometimes he was one of several recipients." She waited again for the judge to indicate he was ready for her to go on.

"We don't know, Judge Affonco, whether there was additional relevant email traffic or text messages among board members, or for that matter to board members from third parties, which were never copied to Mr. Siljadzic. We think some of this stuff probably exists. And it was not produced to us. We ask the court to order the defendant to search *each* of the board members' computers and mobile devices—home and work, wherever—for any emails or other communications that have any relation to the case. And produce them to us. Seven board members."

Alicia paused for another moment, then added, "We're relying on good faith here, Judge. We are not yet at the point of asking for a forensic analysis of each computer hard drive to determine whether and when emails were erased." She sat.

"Mr. Sorowski, you care to respond?"

Tad Sorowski recognized the validity of Santana's request. "Your Honor, I will request each member of the board of school directors to examine his or her computer or similar device, that is, any computer on which he or she might have transacted school board business, and to produce copies of any communications that relate to the matters in litigation."

The judge smiled. "Well stated, Mr. Sorowski. And Ms. Santana, will that do?"

"I accept Mr. Sorowski's word. Yes, Judge, I think that will do."

From his back row in the courtroom, Sam wondered why it was that litigation did not proceed so smoothly when he was involved.

By late spring, Francine Loughlin had edged well away from the precipice of despair. On extended absence from work and still rarely leaving the yellow house on Baker Street, except to sit on her porch or stake the tomato plants in her garden, she found salvation in Barry's steady embrace. Barry LaPorte was with her at every free moment.

"You have saved me," he told her as they brewed coffee and warmed croissants in the toaster oven one morning in the first week of June, the sun already shining through the east window. A crystal pendant hung in front of the window and cast tiny rainbows about the kitchen.

She couldn't believe he was saying that. "No, silly, it's the other way round."

"I mean it, Frannie. I feel happier than I've ever been. I came to you in your grief and you opened your arms to me."

"Oh, Barry. Not just my arms. I have opened my heart to you too. My full heart."

"Beyond comprehension," he said. "I am the luckiest man. And not to be too crass, let's not forget your legs," he could not resist adding, as the coffee bubbled and sputtered and the last of it percolated into the top chamber of the pot. "You have opened your legs to me too."

Francine's first reaction was to want to scold Barry, but she did not. She turned off the gas and poured for them both and brought the croissants on plates over to the table. Yes, she thought, she had opened her legs too. He had thawed her frozen core and she had become again a woman who could love back and give her body and feel it all. She had traveled a long distance.

"Anytime," she said quietly. "Arms, heart, and legs. Body and soul." She pried open the spout to the half-pint carton of half-and-half, smiling at him the whole while, and dribbled a few drops of cream into both cups. "Do you know, Barry, how much gratitude I feel?"

"Maybe on the same scale as the way I feel." He brought his cup to his lips, blew on it, put it down, and picked up a croissant.

She watched him shimmering through the steam of their coffees, as he tore off the end of his croissant and used a spoon to spread black currant jam. She watched him bring the croissant to his mouth and she watched him chew and his tongue retrieve a bit of currant jam escaping to the side of his lip.

"What are you looking at?" he asked.

She did not answer with words, just continued to smile, her heart warm and wobbly.

"Finish your breakfast," she said at last, "and get yourself off to work."

But not long after he was gone, Francine fell backward into her tunnel of dark thoughts. She had heard about her daughter's confidences with the school principal. The stories clouded her vision, like a grimy windshield. She could not see through to any clear truth on the other side.

She paid little attention to other things she heard. Ricky Stillwell had won an early ruling in his First Amendment case against the school, but then had dropped the suit; Gayle Peters had been fired, and was suing the school; lawyers and the miasmal world outside churned on, as if those things were important.

She finished her coffee and washed the dishes and went upstairs and ironed three of Barry's shirts, pressing hard and squirting steam liberally, and this activity calmed her mind. She then took a bath. She soaked for close to an hour, her head half submerged, her mind drifting, and as the bath water cooled she tried to imagine what would happen if she encountered Ricky Stillwell sometime in the future. But she did not have the power to imagine what she might say to him.

The employer is at fault because one of its agents committed an action based on discriminatory animus that was intended to cause, and did in fact cause, an adverse employment decision.

Staub v. Proctor Hospital, 131 S.Ct. 1186, 1193 (2011)

On the day after Ricky's February hearing at the Fred I. Parker Courthouse in Burlington, after listening to the compromised principal testify, Clara Stillwell, in a fury, had written an email. She sent it to three of her colleagues on the Montpelier board of school directors. They were the three who, she felt, would understand. She did not include the board chair, Charlie Siljadzic, a Muslim from Sarajevo who had arrived in Montpelier in 1994 with the first wave of Bosnian refugees, ethnic and cleansed. He, she felt, would not understand.

One time at a school board meeting there was spirited discussion of the new ESL program—English as a Second Language—at the high school. Siljadzic, a strong proponent of the program, used the word *cosmopolitan* to describe both Montpelier and Sarajevo, his beloved city before the Balkan wars, and perhaps he was also sketching his vision of the way the world ought to be. Clara didn't like the word. It sounded un-American and atheistic and materialistic, like a glossy magazine celebrating the hedonistic life. Her distaste for that word was emblematic of the reasons why Siljadzic was not part of Clara's confidential email circle.

Thus, when all relevant documents were finally produced and delivered to Alicia Santana, as Judge Affonco had ordered, included among the computer records of Clara Stillwell and the three trusted board members was the email sent by Stillwell on the day after the hearing in her son's case. That email had never made its way to Siljadzic's inbox, had never before been disclosed to Sorowski, and therefore was a delicious surprise, waiting to be discovered by Alicia Santana.

In her electronic epistle, Clara Stillwell had urged her fellow board members, those within her sympathetic circle, to oust Gayle Peters for "polluting the minds and morals" of high school students with her "anti-Christian homosexual agenda."

In her Chamber Street office, Alicia Santana opened the envelope from Tad Sorowski and scanned through its contents. It did not take long to find Clara Stillwell's missive. She read it three times, her grin spreading wider around the room, and then she yelled out to Sam. There in plain view was Clara Stillwell's righteous hatred of lesbians, visible as the ink on the page.

Her leg vibrating under her desk, her heart pumping, she phoned Gayle. "Are you ready for this, Gayle? We found a smoking gun." She read the letter aloud. Sam had come into the room, hovering at her shoulder, listening. "Gayle, this changes it all. Fucking Clara, she handed it to us. We have Monica Lewinsky's blue dress, and it's stained with Clara's venom."

"Hardly a pretty image," said Gayle, but Alicia could hear her chuckling nonetheless. Acute as always, Gayle then inquired whether Clara Stillwell's motives would necessarily be imputed to the board as a whole. "What if," she asked, "a majority of the board showed no improper bias? Then don't we have the same hurdle? Does Clara's venom infect them all?"

"Oh, good point, very good point. But not a problem. Gayle, there's no way the board can show that its decision was not somehow *tainted* by Clara Stillwell's prejudices. Look, we might have had a difficult case before, right? We were faced with having to persuade a jury to *infer* bias based on the circumstantial evidence—the way the school district had coddled heterosexual staff with loose tongues. Not to say you had a loose—you understand. But now no inference needs to be teased out. Right? We've got homophobia straight out of the horse's mouth. We've got them by the balls."

Metaphors mixed in a cosmopolitan stew. Or goulash.

Tad Sorowski, no fool, knew it too. He used different words to describe the same situation to his client.

The school board huddled together in executive session at its next meeting, and gave Sorowski broad authority to negotiate a settlement. They were prepared to cave.

Clara Stillwell was not present at the meeting. The portly board chair had spoken with her earlier. "It might be easiest," he told her kindly, "if you did not participate." He was considering her feelings as much as the need for the board to act cleanly and decisively, without conflict of interest. Religious fervor was not conducive to compromise.

Negotiations quickly ensued and the parties reached an agreement. Gayle Peters would submit a letter of resignation effective the following Friday. She would receive a lump sum payment equivalent to a full year's salary, plus her attorney's fees, and the board would pay her health benefits through the following school year, unless she first obtained benefits elsewhere.

Before the ink was dry on the separation agreement, Tad Sorowski sent a letter to Alicia. He opened with a compliment. "I write, first, to offer congratulations for what we can both agree is a legal victory for Gayle Peters in her suit against the School District."

Then an admonition: "I hope you and Ms. Peters will appreciate that Clara Stillwell's views, as expressed in her communication to some of her fellow Board members, do not represent the views of any other Board member or of the Board as an institution. You will further appreciate that any suggestion to the contrary would be considered defamatory."

Then came an appeal followed by sage advice: "I would like to ask that you and your client maintain the confidentiality of this information. I respectfully suggest that keeping the information confidential will inure to the benefit not only of the Board and Ms. Stillwell, but also of Ms. Peters, who should not wish it to be publicly known that her settlement with the Board was achieved as a result of the disclosure of Ms. Stillwell's febrile communication rather than through her own salutary qualities."

And finally a defense of his own probity: "I trust you understand that I was not aware of the existence of the offending email communication until it was produced as a consequence of the computer file searches undertaken at your request at the last court hearing. I was surprised, and needless to say, aggrieved."

"Dear Tad," she responded. "I take you at your word. I see no reason for Clara Stillwell's letter to be made public, but my client can decide for herself. Thanks and be well."

Indeed, the settlement was a good result for Gayle Peters and her attorney. But salvaging Gayle's torn reputation was another thing. "I can't stay in Vermont," she told Alicia. "No district is going to hire me. I'm poison."

"You may be right, Gayle. I'm so sorry. What do you think you'll do?"

"I have to move somewhere where I don't have a past." But they both knew that in the age of the Internet you can't escape your past.

Part IV
Arguing Prayer

In early July, Sam Jacobson finally received notice from the Second Circuit Court of Appeals in New York City that oral argument would be held on October 12 in the matter of *Lucy Cross v. Town of Jefferson*, the case challenging prayer at town meeting.

He had been in a dejected mood. Everyone was. Donna was stressed with work. Her clients were always needy, but that was expected and acceptable. What was not acceptable was a hostile work environment, especially within state government, especially within the branch of government charged with vocational counseling.

Although most of the front-line counselors were women, the culture of an old boys' club pervaded the agency. When she raised the subject with her boss, the deputy commissioner, he accused her of being too damned sensitive.

"I'm not saying that because you're a woman," he then had the balls to say. "Donna, you just need to give slack to people who've been here a long time, and they're used to doing things a certain way. People tease. That doesn't make them old boys."

She reminded him she had been there a long time, too. To which he replied with utter inconsistency, "Maybe *too* long, Donna."

"You're kidding?" she said.

"Yes, I was kidding," snapped the deputy commissioner, without a smile. Donna relayed it all to Sam, who became apoplectic, which was no help to her at all.

Their daughter Sarah had been taciturn since their visit in Providence in April. She was wrapped in her own affairs and seemed uninterested in her parents' endeavors. Ricky Stillwell was still out of town, with that camping van somewhere in the South. Clara Stillwell now chose to ignore Sam as a heretic; Carver Stillwell never spoke to Sam anyway. Lucy Cross was ill with rheumatism and isolated up in Jefferson Center, most unlikely to travel to New York for the court argument. Sam heard Francine Loughlin was still deep in grief and still on leave from work, but getting support from that cop friend of hers.

The news from Washington was horrible. The news from the Middle East and North Africa was worse than horrible. Even the public's mythologized heroes, overinflated by the press, were punctured: randy General Petraeus undressed by his embedded biographer; dopey Tour de France Armstrong lanced by his own mendacity; avuncular Cosby exposed as a man who surreptitiously drugged women so he could fuck with them. What a miserable time.

And Sam's law practice? Usual work for an agricultural lender trying to protect its collateral when its loans went south, which sometimes entailed foreclosure on the farm and the loss of another treasure of Vermont's working landscape. Representing employees fired for alleged incompetence or bad behavior; and employers hoping to fire incompetent and badly behaving employees. Nurses and day care centers fighting the state in their licensing proceedings.

He had one client, a local veterinarian, whose license was in jeopardy because the method he used to euthanize certain cats, by intracardial injection, failed to meet national guidelines promulgated by a veterinarians' association. Another client was a graduate student in pharmacology who had been dismissed from the University of Vermont for submitting falsified data in a research project.

Sam had been able to convince the university, and the press, that the student's malfeasance was instigated by the professor in charge of the lab, and they reached a settlement permitting the student to continue in the program. Whereupon the student, celebrating her victory that night, got drunk on vodka martinis, hopped into her car, lost control going down Burlington's Pearl Street toward the lake, swerved onto the sidewalk, and hit and killed a pedestrian, who happened to be the husband of the university's provost.

And Sam represented the Montpelier City Council in an eminent domain proceeding, when the city administration sought to condemn the building at the end of Sproul Street that housed Beverage Discount King and Redemption Center in order to construct, straight through the unhappily situated beverage building, what was officially known as the Central Vermont Multi-Modal Route, and unofficially known as The Bike Path. Green bike path lovers were pitted against holy bottle redeemers.

So the notice from the Second Circuit was a welcome distraction. For a Montpelier lawyer, it was a big deal to argue a case before the Second Circuit, like being called from the farm league team to play with the big boys in the Major Leagues.

Sam was eager to share and went out to meet his loyal partner for lunch, and found her sitting at a table on the brick sidewalk in front of the Sacred Grounds Café. It was hot and sunny, even sticky, and the awning over the tables provided welcome shade. They ate bagel sandwiches. Sam had his usual dark coffee, while Alicia drank an iced chai latté.

Alicia was thrilled. "I'm coming to New York to watch, if it's all right with you," she told him, knowing it was. "Barb and I are planning a New York trip anyway, to celebrate our ten-year anniversary of moving in together. Did you know?"

Sam shook his head.

"Ten years of shared housekeeping and shoveling! We talked about going to the city on Columbus Day weekend. So this is perfect. We want to check out the High Line," referring to the park on the old elevated rail spur on the West Side. "But I want to hear the arguments and maybe I can talk Barb into it too."

"Fabulous," he said, his mood improving another notch, pleased both to have Alicia with him at court, and to be included in her celebration with Barb. "I would like that very much, partner." He nursed his coffee. "Maybe I'll ask Sarah if she'll come over on the train from Providence."

Alicia smiled at that idea. "You might turn that kid onto law school yet, Sam. She's got the head for it."

Sam nodded to acknowledge her point, but he left it alone. He had had more than one fruitless discussion on the subject with Sarah.

He asked Alicia how Barb was doing.

"Frazzled," Alicia answered, "and glad summer is here. June was tough at school." The final month of the school year had been chaotic, she explained. Physics teacher John Carruthers had served as interim principal while the search for Gayle Peters's replacement was underway.

Carruthers had previously sat on various committees and headed up the design of a revised school-wide science curriculum, but he had little administrative experience. And he was in the midst of a ravaging divorce from his ravaging wife. Responsibility to keep things running at the school fell largely on Barb. She was not given a pay raise.

"On the other hand," Alicia continued, "Barb is kind of relieved to have Gayle Peters gone. She always admired Gayle, right? But there's some quality to her character that made Barb anxious, like there's a veil hiding the real Gayle Peters inside. She could never quite describe it." Sam couldn't describe it either, but he could relate to Barb's ambivalence. "Well, you know, Barb's a bit anxious anyway."

Across the street, Sandra Winchester, the biology teacher, emerged from the toy store with her well-fed two-year-old in tow. Alicia, who had interviewed her briefly in preparation for Peters's case, waved hello. Winchester and son crossed over. "My law partner, Sam Jacobson," said Alicia. "Sam, this is Sandra Winchester—Sandra, not Sandy, right?—one of the teachers at the high school."

With her son on her hip, Winchester leaned in, smiling, and shook Sam's hand. "Mr. Jacobson," she began to say.

"Call me Sam, please." She had stunning good looks, flaxen hair, a warm and trusting smile.

"This is my boy, Weston. You can say hi to them, Wes." But he was shy and he didn't. He tried to tuck his head under his mother's arm.

"Sam," she continued, her smile fading, "may I tell you something? I think Ricky Stillwell is a great kid. But what he said to Kerry Pearson? That wasn't okay. I'm sorry, I'm being awfully bold, and I really have no right to butt in like this? But I just don't understand how you could defend what he wrote to Kerry. I was shocked. We all were, everybody at the school."

Alicia took the quick bait. "No, he didn't defend what Ricky wrote to Kerry. That's not it."

"It's not it?"

Sam said, "So, you know, we try to distinguish between defending someone's right to say something, and defending the thing itself. But I do take your point. I didn't like what Ricky said any better than you did." He wiped his brow in the heat. "Sandra, did you know Kerry well?"

Sandra Winchester looked intently at Sam, and set her boy down on the brick parquet. "Yes."

Weston started to pull away, his eye back on the toy store on the other side of Chamber. But she held on to his hand and held on to Sam's gaze for several seconds more, and the silence grew uncomfortable.

Then she said, "You're saying Ricky had the right to say things. I understand that. But did he have the right to say those particular things? Such hateful and hurtful things?"

"Well, we think so," Sam answered. "I, too, am sorry about how hurtful it was."

"Can't we make distinctions?" she queried. "Must it be all or nothing?"

"It is *not* all or nothing," said Alicia. "The First Amendment does not protect slanders or obscenities or what courts call true threats. And some other categories. It's not like all speech is considered free in that sense. Like, you know, you can't yell *Fire* in a crowded theater is a classic example. This wasn't any of those things."

In a tremulous voice, she said, "I don't know. We've just got to open our hearts to everyone, in all our shapes, whatever our sexes and genders. We are one family, you know? We all share the same *Homo sapiens* DNA."

"Sandra, you are so right about that," said Alicia.

Sandra let Weston pull her away, said, "Pleased to meet you," to Sam, and left them.

"Shit," said Sam. Alicia nodded in agreement. "She is no dumb cookie. But you thought she was a dumb cookie at first, didn't you, Sam?"

"No," he said. But he was forced to smile weakly at Alicia, as he knew she knew he was lying.

"Did you know," Alicia said to him, "most of us also have a bit of Neanderthal DNA too? Everyone except for Africans."

"I've heard something about that, but I didn't know the part about Africans. Is that right?"

"That's right. Wherever Neanderthals lived, and that did not include Africa, we *Homo sapiens* apparently had sex with them." Smiling broadly at Sam, she added, "But who's to know whether we had *gay* sex with them?"

Walking over from the courthouse and wearing his trademark bowtie, Judge Dennis Affonco, ducked into the shade under the awning to greet Sam and Alicia. He was on a break from trial, he said, this one involving a boundary dispute between two property owners each adamantly claiming the rights to the same useless strip of woodlot.

Turning to Alicia, he said, "Glad you settled that employment discrimination case, Ms. Santana. Better to resolve it out of court. Would have gotten a bit ugly, I think."

Alicia, conscious not to drop the pronouns from her own sentences lest the judge think she was imitating him, agreed. "Do you remember, Judge, that you ordered discovery of emails kept on school board members' computers? An incriminating email did turn up, written by one of the board members. That's what turned the case. It was a pretty vicious email."

Judge Affonco gave a friendly smile, but did not want to hear more. "Good thing. Would have gotten ugly. Better keep going on my midday constitutional. Don't want to fall asleep on the bench."

As the judge disappeared down the street, Alicia asked Sam: "What the hell is a midday constitutional? Does it have anything to do with constitutional law?"

"Fuck do I know. Never know what the judge is talking about," said Sam, dropping the pronoun.

Just as there are sound and convincing interpretations of literature as well as frivolous or incompetent readings, there are also skilled and inept interpretations of legal rights. Sound legal practice is not primarily a matter of mechanical rule application;

instead, it requires the exercise of sound judgment, studied expertise, and common sense in interpreting and applying the law. . . . Too many people, misled by simplistic metaphors likening judges to umpires and the law to a rule book in a game, seem to think that a judge can just apply the law to the facts without her own wisdom and judgment playing a role.

Richard Thompson Ford, *Rights Gone Wrong: How Law Corrupts the Struggle for Equality* (Farrar, Straus and Giroux, 2011), 130-31

The Second Circuit Court of Appeals resides in the Learned Hand Courthouse, a quite-new marble tower, located behind the old courthouse buildings on Foley Square in lower Manhattan. The building gives the paradoxical impression of both light and substance. Across the street from its entrance is a small playground and park, Columbus Park.

The park borders on Chinatown, a few congested blocks of tenements, produce markets with crates of cabbages spilling onto the sidewalks, apothecaries, restaurants with crisp roasted ducks hanging in steamy windows, trinket shops, blocked traffic, and a throng of pedestrians: a headache of incessant motion, noise and clutter.

Despite the surrounding chaos, it was peaceful in the park, where Barb Laval in her cantaloupe-colored fleece sat on a bench watching a dozen elderly women perform t'ai chi with exquisitely calculated movements.

A smattering of children played basketball on the nearby court. The noise from surrounding streets seemed distant. Barb soaked up the warm October sun, closed her eyes, and imagined her body expanding and contracting like the t'ai chi movements. She felt gratitude for the good life around her. She felt gratitude for Alicia, who was presently with Sam inside the courthouse. And yet, with her eyes closed, she frowned.

She sat on the bench in the park, and did not join Alicia and Sam in the courthouse, because she was sick of the law. At another time, she would have watched the oral arguments in the town meeting prayer case. She had heard about the heap of abuse piled on Lucy Cross and she was sympathetic. She also knew from Alicia that the case might become an Important First Amendment Case.

She didn't understand it all, though Alicia had answered some of Barb's questions. The First Amendment says *Congress* shall make no law respecting an establishment of religion. It says nothing about the states or towns. But the constitutional amendments adopted after the Civil War shifted the balance among the states, the people, and the national polity.

So the First Amendment's limits on Congress were applied to the states as well because, Alicia said, the Fourteenth Amendment forbade States—and political subdivisions of the States, like the Town of Jefferson—from depriving people of liberty without due process. Including the liberties of the First Amendment! It was a neat package. And the Town of Jefferson, Alicia explained, established an official religion by holding prayer at town meeting. And that deprived Lucy Cross of her liberty.

Was that it? Where, Barb wondered, did the due process piece come in?

The whole thing was perplexing. Barb thought about the people in Jefferson who wanted to pray at town meeting. Couldn't Lucy Cross just ignore the prayer? Or hang about outside until the prayer was over?

Barb remembered as a child reciting the Lord's Prayer every morning at her primary school in St. Lambert, the suburb where her family then lived on the South Shore of the St.

Lawrence River facing Montreal. Not reciting really, more like incoherent mumbling. *Forgive us our trespasses* did not carry a clear meaning for a child of seven.

She remembered learning, at some point in those years, that to trespass meant to go on someone else's property without permission. She never did *that*, she thought, so why was she supposed to ask God to forgive her? She had asked her Grade 4 teacher about this, but the teacher scowled and told her never to question God's judgment. It was a public school, an English-language protestant public school. The Catholics had their own schools. Canada made do without an Establishment Clause. Barb never felt that the city of St. Lambert deprived her of liberty—not in that particular way, anyway.

But there was more on her mind, as she felt the sun in the park and the quiet movements of the t'ai chi dancers. What soured her on the legal world, Alicia's world, were the crusades of Gayle Peters and Ricky Stillwell.

A couple of years earlier, Barb remembered, Alicia had read a book by a law professor called *Rights Gone Wrong*. They had gone up to Montreal for a long weekend. It was in fact on Columbus Day two years ago, she now recalled, the holiday known in Canada as Thanksgiving.

On Rue St. Viatur, they bought sesame bagels still steaming hot from the brick oven. It was a Saturday, the Sabbath, and the street was crowded with orthodox Jews in black satin jackets and stiff fur hats, surrounding Barb and Alicia as they chewed hot sweet bagels and turned south on St. Lawrence Boulevard. Alicia was going on about the book, as she sometimes did with books that excited her, but Barb had never grasped what it was really about.

Ah, she realized here in Columbus Park in another city, two years later to the day—the professor must have been writing about the tribulations of Montpelier High School. For the federal court had ruled that Ricky Stillwell could not be punished by the school for calling out his lesbian classmate as a sinner, an exercise of *right* so damaging that she took her life. As for Principal Peters, the school was not permitted to fire her for a breach of professional boundaries because just one of its board members, a fundamentalist Christian, may have violated her *right* to a workplace free of discrimination against lesbians.

Rights gone wrong. The school she loved had lost every which way.

Alicia said the cases all tied together. She said the principle was that every person should be treated with equal concern for their dignity. If heterosexual staff could be open about relationship issues in the public school, the theory of equal concern required that gay staff be afforded the same latitude. Anything less, Alicia said, was an injury to dignity.

Same with the Town of Jefferson. It was required to treat Lucy Cross with equal concern, and that meant affording the same level of respect for her fundamental beliefs on moral and religious matters as any other person in town. Anyone can pray, in church or at home or on the town green. But the town should not be permitted to impose a prayer on all its residents, one size fits all. And that is what happens when the local Christian minister is called to the podium at every town meeting.

Okay, a perplexed Barb had asked her again, but what about Ricky Stillwell and Kerry Pearson? How do you decide whose dignity is more important?

They had spoken about this one winter night, in their bed under the quilt, many months earlier. That was before the hearing in federal court when Gayle Peters first revealed her private palavers with Kerry. At the time, as Barb recalled, Alicia seemed to agree there was a balance to be found, with free speech on one side and privacy on the other.

That conversation had been tempered by tears and ended in lovemaking, and now in the park Barb lost herself momentarily in the rippling recollection. The sensation passed, and her mind turned back disagreeably to the conflict.

When they talked about this more recently, Alicia didn't equivocate. Kerry had the right to be herself, to be her lesbian self. "But Ricky," she had said with her hands in the air in a gesture of exasperation, "Ricky had the right to voice his own views, to speak as an autonomous person. We"—who is *we*, wondered Barb? Did Alicia mean the school district, or all of us?—"we have the moral obligation to treat Ricky with equal concern, the same concern we must show for all individuals who express personal moral views, whether we agree or not. Right? If we censor him, if we punish him for his speech, then we trample on his dignity and we violate his civil liberties." Alicia had glared at Barb in her fierce way.

"Those liberties don't feel so civil to me," Barb had told Alicia.

Alicia had also explained that Sam did not share her view. He believed you advance the best legal arguments for your client, regardless of any ethical theory. Alicia was impatient with Sam's cynicism. "We must choose our clients with care," she insisted. "And the strength of our legal arguments derives from the underlying theory."

Alicia could be so self-assured about her causes, maybe even self-righteous, like a mirror image of Clara Stillwell. She could be critical, too. Even about trivial things, Barb worried, hunched forward in her fleece with her elbows on her knees and her fingers on her temples.

They had a wall calendar from the Sierra Club that hung on a kitchen cupboard. In the little space for October 27, below the stunning photograph of some California beeches, Barb had written *Appointment with Dr. Vassar, 10 a.m.*

Alicia noticed this a couple of days ago when she opened the cupboard to get a can of tomato sauce. "Why the hell don't you just write *Vassar at 10*?" she asked Barb, who was seated at the kitchen table reviewing their last bank statement.

"What? Why?" said Barb, hurt.

"What you wrote takes up the whole space, Barb. It's silly. You know Dr. Vassar is a doctor. So you don't need to write *doctor*. Let alone *appointment*. Right?"

"But you don't even use this calendar for your stuff," said Barb defensively. "Why does it matter to you, Alicia?"

And Alicia said something about the principle of it, and never mind, no big deal, as she opened the can and used a rubber spatula to scoop the tomato sauce into a pan of sautéed onions and garlic and celery.

But Barb did mind, and the argument was a big deal. How did a wall of separation come between them?

On the park bench, Barb was crying silently. A t'ai chi woman noticed and walked over and peered into Barb's face. The woman said, "You okay, lady? Sad? Sunny day."

Barb smiled at her and they shook hands.

Inside the courthouse tower, the Montpelier lawyers were 45 minutes early and they headed to the courtroom to watch the argument scheduled before the town meeting prayer case. Members of the press congregated in the adjacent hallway. The prayer case had generated public interest, especially after Lionel Fox, the high-profile, press-savvy lawyer with the national organization, Americans for Traditional Values, stepped in to represent the Town of Jefferson, Vermont, once the appeal was filed. Sam ignored them.

As with most cases presented to federal courts of appeal, a panel of three judges was convened to hear the morning's arguments and decide the appeals. Today, the judge in the middle, the senior member of the panel, squinting over his elfish grin, was Guido Calabresi, the great law and economics scholar and former dean of the Yale Law School. Sam was pleased to have Judge Calabresi on the panel because he was considered to be a broad-minded liberal who, Sam imagined, may be more likely than some other judges on the Circuit to have a generous, nurturing attitude toward the Establishment Clause.

Also, he knew the judge.

As a student at the Yale Law School many years earlier, he had studied torts with Professor Calabresi. Sam came to the law school with a college degree in philosophy, two years working in a bicycle shop, and a childhood untouched by the darker side of the legal system. He knew next to nothing about the law when he began.

So he had learned at the knee of Professor Calabresi, finding beauty and occasional logic in the slicing of common law torts. But knowing the judge when he was a law professor had no sway here in the world of the courtroom. On one other occasion in recent years, he had appeared before Judge Calabresi to argue a technical case about health benefits; when Sam sat down he felt grilled and shredded by the judge with the elfish grin.

Alicia nudged him with a sharp elbow and nodded toward the bench. Sam realized that the argument, the one preceding theirs, was about ferrets.

The lawyer at the podium identified herself as representing New York City Friends of Ferrets. Sam gathered that this noble organization had challenged a New York City Department of Health policy, barring people from owning ferrets as household pets in the city. The policy also required euthanasia of any ferret found to have bitten a human, without first providing a hearing to the pet's owner.

This policy, asserted the organization's lawyer, was unconstitutional—a violation of the Equal Protection Clause!—because the city treated ferret owners differently from, say, dog owners.

City counsel then approached the podium and referred to studies showing that ferrets were inclined to attack infants, with unhappy results, and that the mammal was also prone to contracting rabies which, according to some trusted experts, could be confirmed only by killing the creature forthwith and examining its brain. This had something to do with the uncertainty of the "viral shedding period" for ferrets, unlike, say, dogs. So the policy's different treatment of ferrets (and their owners) and dogs (and their owners), said New York City's lawyer, had a rational basis and therefore must be upheld.

The lawyer for the city finished, and the three judges leaned in and quietly conferred for a moment. Judge Calabresi said, "Thank you, counselors. We have previously reviewed and reached a preliminary decision in this case based on your written submissions. The oral arguments have not altered our views. Judge Rothberger"—and he turned to the judge sitting to his left—"will read our decision from the bench."

The process was unusual, and the unusual became surreal as Judge Fritz Rothberger, an old-school conservative, former corporate counsel, announced the decision in *basso profundo* Viennese-accented rhyme.

Since ferrets bite babies
And may infect them with rabies,
New York will take pains
To examine their brains.

But for dogs there's no need.
Just put them in cages.
Their behavior will show
If their bite is contagious.

If a dog is infected,
It will go quite insane.
But a ferret will not.
You must dissect its brain.

We apply minimal scrutiny,
As you know from our cases.
A law will survive if
There's a rational basis.

Each species here has
Its own path of infection.
Hence no abridgement
Of equal protection.

So, Friends of the Ferret,
Your claim has no merit.
Grin and bear it.

"The next case," the bailiff immediately proclaimed in booming monotone, as if nothing strange had occurred, "is *Lucy Cross versus Town of Jefferson*." She read out the docket number.

The unnerved lawyers on the ferret case scrambled to clear their papers, and Sam stood up with his folder of notes and photocopied case law. As the appellant, having lost at the federal district court in Vermont, he would give the first argument, to be followed by the famous Fox with Traditional Values.

Sam was apprehensive, thrown off-kilter by the court's irreverence in the case just heard. As he approached the podium, he glanced behind him for final encouragement from Alicia. He met her warm eyes and at the same moment noticed his daughter Sarah, sitting a few seats back. She had not told him she would come. But there she sat, beaming at him.

Then, like an optical trick played in an Escher drawing, his focus shifted again. A few rows behind Sarah in the gallery, a vision of Ricky Stillwell emerged, here in the Court of Appeals in New York, here to watch his argument.

Did his audience observe the uncharacteristic bounce in the step of the aging barrister, the lift in his shoulders as he placed his hands on each side of the podium and faced the panel of judges?

In light of the unambiguous and unbroken history of more than 200 years, there can be no doubt that the practice of opening legislative sessions with prayer has become part of the fabric of our society. To invoke Divine guidance on a public body entrusted with making the laws is not, in these circumstances, an "establishment" of religion or a step toward establishment; it is simply a tolerable acknowledgement of beliefs widely held among the people of this country.

Marsh v. Chambers, 463 U.S. 783, 792 (1983)

"Good morning, your Honors, may it please the court." Sam Jacobson recited the traditional verbiage, but before he got in another word he was interrupted.

Judge Calabresi asked how this case differed from *Marsh v. Chambers.*

Sam knew he'd be summoned to wade into *Marsh*. It was a 1983 decision of the Supreme Court that upheld as constitutional the Nebraska state legislature's practice of opening each legislative day with prayer. If *Marsh* were the controlling precedent for the Jefferson town meeting, Lucy Cross had lost her case.

In *Marsh*, the Supreme Court effectively carved out a special favored status for legislative prayers, which otherwise would surely have been struck down had the court applied its usual test (known as the *Lemon* test) for evaluating whether a government body's association with a religious practice was constitutional.

The *Lemon* test asks, among other things, whether the purpose of the association is religious or secular, and it is hard to dispute that the purpose of holding religious prayers before legislative sessions is religious. But *Marsh* ignored *Lemon*, and the Supreme Court permitted the prayers. Sam had no respect for the shoddy reasoning behind the decision. But shoddy or not, it is now the law, the supreme law, and he was required to give reasons why it should not control the outcome of Lucy Cross's case.

He reached to tug on the beard that no longer graced his chin, and told the court there were at least four reasons why *Marsh* did not govern the present case.

"First," he said, "the prayer given to open the annual town meeting in Jefferson is *sectarian*. The town moderator invites the same pastor from the same Christian church, year after year, who prays to the Father, the Son, and the Holy Spirit. This practice impermissibly endorses one religion over another. That is a critical distinguishing point."

Sam held his hands in front of him, beckoning the panel of three to follow his lead. "The Nebraska legislative prayer, by contrast, was considered by the court to be *non*-sectarian. Indeed, the court noted that while earlier prayers were explicitly Christian, the clergyman had removed all references to Christ after a complaint in 1980 from a Jewish legislator. *Marsh*, your

Honors, does not permit sectarian prayer, or prayer expressly invoking particular Christian tenets."

In truth, Sam detested this argument; it should not matter how sectarian a prayer is, and nobody wanted to give judges the warrant to scrutinize the content of prayers and decide which of them is sufficiently kosher to satisfy the First Amendment. But he had to make the argument, because the sectarian-nonsectarian distinction was drawn, albeit obliquely, in *Marsh*.

Judge Calabresi cleared his throat and interjected. "The court's concern in *Marsh* seems to me less about how sectarian a prayer is, than whether the occasion is used to proselytize, that is to say, to advance one or disparage another religion. I am not sure, Mr. Jacobson, that every minister who delivers a prayer, no matter how sectarian, is thereby proselytizing his particular brand of religion.

"Or perhaps we should better put the question this way: is the *town* here necessarily proselytizing, or advancing one religion, or disparaging another, if it invites a church minister to deliver a sectarian Christian prayer before the annual meeting?"

Sam scrambled to articulate his thoughts. "Advancing one religion over others, yes, Judge Calabresi, that is correct, that's a critical point in *Marsh*. But the *Marsh* court also noted that the prayers at the Nebraska legislature were nonsectarian. These points, I think, are connected in the following way."

With his arms out in front, like a traffic cop, Sam expounded: "It is the long-term sectarian practice, which has not changed in the Town of Jefferson over the course of many years, that has the *effect* of advancing one branch of Christian faith over other religions. I think that is what the Court in *Marsh* says is forbidden under the Establishment Clause. We would have the same problem," Sam riskily supposed, "if a town brought in a rabbi every year, without fail, to deliver a Hebrew blessing. While Jews are not known as proselytizers, such a practice would not satisfy *Marsh*."

"I wonder," replied the judge, amused at the thought. "What if once in every five years, a Christian minister delivers a sectarian prayer at the town meeting, undeniably sectarian, we can agree on this, yes? And in the other four years there are a variety of other invocations, based on different religious faiths and even secular beliefs? That is, let us suppose, the town officials rotate among the faiths and traditions. Would you still say that the delivery of the sectarian Christian prayer constitutes *establishment*?"

"Judge Calabresi, I submit even in those circumstances, there are reasons why the practice you have described should be found unconstitutional. I will try to state those reasons. But I must first emphasize that the practice you have described is very far from the case we have today, where the same minister in the Town of Jefferson gives the same prayer every year, and it is a sectarian prayer." Keep hammering the point.

"As I mentioned, and this is undisputed evidence in the record, each year the minister asks for guidance from the Father, the Son, and the Holy Spirit." Just as Sam Jacobson was now asking for guidance from the three deities on the bench in front of him.

Sitting on the stiff oak bench in the gallery behind the podium where her father stood, Sarah Jacobson craned forward to hear. Behind her, someone muffled a cough. She glanced around, and was surprised to recognize Ricky Stillwell, who offered her a small and skittish smile.

Almost a year had passed since the Kerry Pearson tragedy. Sarah's disdain had softened over time. Her father's observation that Ricky acted from love was lodged in her conscience. She could not help herself and smiled broadly back at Ricky. She moved around to his bench and sidled along next to him. "I'm glad to see you," Sarah whispered, with a gentle poke to his ribs. "We'll catch up when this thing's over."

On second thought, she should not have been surprised at Ricky's presence. She knew he was in New York now, studying at the university only a few blocks from Foley Square. And she also recalled hearing at some point that Ricky had been following this prayer case. But she felt just the smallest disturbance and she tried to locate the reason. Was it because her father must have invited Ricky and maybe had been discussing the case with him, but not with her? Or that her father hadn't told her that Ricky would be here?

On the other hand, she realized soberly that she had never confirmed with her father that she herself would come to watch the argument. Grow up, she told herself, and turned to look at the young man seated beside her.

His profile reminded her of a classical Greek marble head, except that his lips were real and soft. He did not turn; he was focused on Sam's debate with the judge.

The Court is forbidden by the Constitution to consider anything but concrete cases, involving the real interests of particular litigants. In a civilization growing less human all the time, with budgets beyond the grasp of men and weapons that can wipe out continents, surely there is special value in an institution that focuses on the individual. . . . Argument itself reflects the distinctions of the judicial process. It is so much more concentrated and intellectually focused than, for example, a legislative debate. . . . [J]ustices and counsel can deal directly, in [a] curiously intimate way . . . , with the heart of a problem.

Anthony Lewis, *Gideon's Trumpet*
(Vintage Books, 1964), 223-24

"Let me turn to the second reason why *Marsh* is distinguishable." Sam addressed the court, wading deeper into the reeds. "The minister at the Jefferson town meeting is called to pray to the entire gathering of town residents. His prayer is offered for them, the citizens. The legislators in *Marsh*, on the other hand, chose to hold the prayer for their *own* benefit. For constitutional purposes, this distinction is important." Important, but obscure.

"It is one thing," he continued, "for a legislative body to offer a prayer to inspire its own actions, when other members of the public may be present as mere spectators. That's what happened in *Marsh*. That's not an establishment of religion, according to *Marsh*.

"It is another thing entirely for public officials to call the *public* to prayer for *its* benefit. *That* constitutes an establishment. And *that* is what happens at the Jefferson, Vermont, town meeting."

The judges on the bench eyed Sam with skepticism, at least he so interpreted their arched brows and creased foreheads and a distinct frown from Judge Rothberger.

But for the moment they remained politely quiet, and Sam proceeded. "This distinction was made by the Supreme Court in the subsequent case of *Lee v. Weisman*. *Lee v. Weisman* held that prayers delivered at a public high school graduation ceremony were unconstitutional under the First Amendment. Those graduation prayers were delivered supposedly for the benefit of the public—the students, parents and guests.

"This point was noted by Justice Souter in his concurring opinion in *Lee v. Weisman*. Souter stated that the case was not controlled by *Marsh*. It wasn't controlled by *Marsh*, Justice

Souter wrote, because in *Marsh* the legislators invoked spiritual inspiration entirely for their own benefit, without directing any religious message at the citizens—unlike the school graduation prayers. The prayers in *Marsh* were deemed permissible. School graduation prayers are not."

It was a subtle argument. Prayers for the officials' own benefit versus prayers directed at the public; the first permissible, the second not.

Still no interruption from the bench, so he closed the point. "Now, your Honors, unlike the legislative prayers in *Marsh*, but like the prayers in *Lee v. Weisman* in this respect, the prayers delivered at the Jefferson town meetings are precisely intended to invoke spiritual inspiration for the benefit of all town residents who attend the meeting. This constitutes an impermissible establishment of religion."

Bravo, said Alicia to herself, scarcely able to stay seated at counsel table.

Ricky, on the other hand, lanky on his gallery bench, was unmoved by this argument. He still felt that religion had no place in government at all. It should not matter whether prayers were directed inward or outward. The sacred and the profane should not mix. He whispered his point into Sarah's ear.

She could not follow as she also tried to hear the argument up front. But to her surprise she enjoyed the intimacy between them, profane more than sacred, his long leg pressed now against hers, a sweet smell of coffee on his breath, earnestness in his look, his Adam's apple protruding. Good lord, she thought to herself.

❧

"Third." Sam momentarily placed his index finger in the collar of his shirt, giving it a sharp tug, a gesture that was familiar to Sarah. "The third problem with the prayer practice is that it interferes with the citizens' right to vote. The residents of Jefferson, Vermont, as you know, your Honors, attend their town meeting in order to exercise their constitutional right to vote. Town meeting, after all, is the preeminent institution of local democracy in Vermont.

"What is at stake here is the right to deliberate with one's fellow citizens, to elect town officers, and to vote on town business, all without being subjected to an official, government-sponsored religious prayer."

"Excuse me," said Judge Rothberger, noted author of ferret doggerel. "The legislators in Nebraska also surely vote during their legislative sessions. Yet we have held there is no constitutional impediment to the longstanding tradition of holding prayers at the commencement of these sessions. How can the prayers in Vermont be seen to restrict the right to vote when the prayers in Nebraska evidently do not?"

Sam cast about for a moment, nervous and irritable, but miraculously displaying respect and confidence. "I think the difference is the following, Judge Rothberger. Citizens enjoy the constitutional right to vote, grounded in the First Amendment. Legislators, our elected representatives, may have the *duty* to cast votes, but they do not have the constitutional *right* to do so, in their capacity as legislators. The Jefferson prayer practice interferes with citizens, like Lucy Cross, in the exercise of their constitutional right to vote and deliberate on the public business of the town. Government cannot condition the exercise of one constitutional right on a citizen's sacrifice of another."

Sam ran a hand through his unruly hair, and Judge Rothberger inquired: "So Lucy Cross stays at the meeting and votes. She has that right. Where's the sacrifice? What right is she giving up? Explain this to me."

"She would give up the right to participate in a public assembly and to cast her vote in an environment free from an establishment of religion. If the prayer happened, Judge Rothberger. She could avoid the meeting and give up her right to vote, or she could attend the meeting to vote, and give up her right not to be preached to. Citizens cannot be forced to trade one right for another."

"Sounds circular to me," Judge Rothberger muttered.

You're an idiot, Sam was thinking. Sarah could see the look on her father's face, though he was hiding it from the judge. An apparition of Lucy Cross appeared above the bench in Sarah's mind. Lucy raised an arthritic arm with her cane held high and brought it down first on the withered judge, and then on Sam to knock some sense into him, scolding Sam to bring the argument back from the abstract to her, Lucy Cross, the aggrieved plaintiff.

"Pardon me," said Sam as he realized that a moment of silence had passed. "The plaintiff, Lucy Cross—who incidentally could not attend this argument today in New York, as much as she wanted to; she is rather infirm—is a ninety-plus-year-old woman who wants, simply, to do these things like voting that all other residents can do, without having her town invite a Christian minister to pray at her. She is made to feel like a second-class citizen, like an unwanted aunt, at her own town meeting."

Sarah watched Alicia nodding in approval. Alicia then turned to look at the clock on the back wall, and noticed for the first time Sarah and Ricky sitting together in the gallery. Alicia's face lit up in joy. With embarrassment Sarah then realized that Alicia was taking stock of how very close together she and Ricky were sitting.

✎

"Ibelieve you said there was a fourth way in which *Marsh* should be distinguished?" Calabresi again. It was kind of the judge to maintain the thread.

"Yes, thank you, the fourth point is this." Sam tried to breathe slowly. "The *Marsh Court* justified the constitutionality of the Nebraska legislative prayer in large part because it found that the practice has become part of the *fabric* of our society. But commencing town meeting with a prayer is not part of the fabric of modern Vermont society. Few Vermont towns currently follow this practice. The relative *in* frequency of prayer at Vermont town meetings," Sam rolled on, "as well as the robust health of the Vermont town meeting tradition in the absence of invocation prayers, suggests that the *fabric* rationale of *Marsh* has no weight in the present context."

This was an opportunity to invoke a sort of Vermont exceptionalism. But that was precisely the problem with the argument, which Sam suddenly recognized to his dismay, as Judge Rothberger interrupted.

"Hold your horses, Mr. Jacobson," Rothberger said. "The last time I looked, the First Amendment was part of a national constitution. It is a national constitution we are called upon to expound. That's Chief Justice Marshall in *McCulloch v. Maryland*. There are no separate rules for Vermont. I like Vermont too," he added. "My wife and I had a vacation home near Coolidge Notch. We had to give it up when your legislature decided to tax the heck out of vacation properties. But all that's neither here nor there."

Sam indulged the judge by smiling in a way he hoped would convey graciousness.

"The point is this," Rothberger continued, "I don't see how you square your argument about Vermont being special with the principle that the words of the Establishment Clause are interpreted in light of national traditions and practices."

Caught by this thrust, Sam nevertheless salvaged a nugget of his argument. "Judge Rothberger, let me respond by noting that town meetings of this type are not found throughout the nation. There is no *national* tradition, or national fabric, when it comes to town meetings. These are New England town meetings, with the entire citizenry participating in direct democracy. They don't exist elsewhere in the nation, to my knowledge. And they don't even exist any longer in the cities and larger communities in New England. It becomes too cumbersome. So what we have left are the small towns in Vermont, towns like Jefferson. I'm not certain about Coolidge Notch, Judge Rothberger." He almost winked at the judge.

"And," Sam would make his point again, foolish or not, "I suggest to the court that, if there is a fabric to Vermont society, it is comprised of a diversity of religious and irreligious views and a generous respect and tolerance for iconoclasts." He had practiced that phrase. "Even atheists, your Honors."

Behind him, Alicia was grinning once again.

S am's time was up, and all he had done was to answer the single question posed by Judge Calabresi. It was the central question, however, and he could hardly complain the court gave him the time to answer it. He was ready to close, but Judge Calabresi now addressed him. "A principal rationale for the majority's decision in *Marsh* is the original historical understanding of the Establishment Clause by its authors, yes? You haven't addressed this point. Would you do so?"

Sam and Alicia had rehearsed this issue. Chief Justice Warren Burger emphasized in his 1983 opinion in *Marsh* that the framers reached agreement on the language of the Bill of Rights, including the First Amendment, within a few days of Congress authorizing the appointment of paid chaplains. Even James Madison had voted in favor of the chaplain bill. "Clearly the men who wrote the First Amendment Religion Clause," wrote Chief Justice Burger with barely concealed glee, "did not view paid legislative chaplains and opening prayers as a violation of that Amendment."

Marsh was a choice example of "original intent" jurisprudence, a favored approach of those scholars and judges who thought that constitutional law had become dangerously untethered. Chief Justice Burger held with them that the founders' words mean today what they meant in 1789.

"Yes, Judge Calabresi. I appreciate the force of the historical argument. Nonetheless, it does not trump all other considerations. So I would say this: While the original understanding of the First Amendment might support the court's holding in *Marsh*, that holding is limited, as I noted, to nonsectarian prayers, and to practices that do not involve efforts to proselytize or advance one faith over another. It is limited to contexts where legislators hold prayers for their *own* benefit. It is limited to contexts where citizens are not being asked to give up their right to vote if they wish to avoid the prayer.

"We submit that these other factors must and do inform the proper interpretation of the Establishment Clause, *regardless* of the original intent of the founders, to the extent their original intent can even be *divined*." Sam thought he was being clever with this last word, but all three judges sat like sphinxes, apparently unmoved by his rhetorical flourish.

Judge Calabresi politely shut Mr. Jacobson off and invited Lionel Fox to the podium. Fox sprinted forward. He spent much of his allotted twenty minutes reiterating and elaborating upon the original intent approach, discussing religious practices in the colonies and the young nation. Prayers at public meetings of all types were common and accepted. Tradition, fabric, social mores. To permit invocation prayers at such meetings today does not establish a religion, contended Fox, but instead reflects, as *Marsh* held, "a tolerable acknowledgement of beliefs widely held among the people of this country."

Sitting at counsel table, Sam's head was whirling and he had trouble listening. Alicia, next to him, holding a stoic silence at odds with her nature, placed her hand over Sam's under the table and she squeezed his hand, and that physical connection between them restored his equilibrium. And he suspected that for her part, holding Sam's hand grounded her enough to stop her from rising in her seat and belting out TRADITION! at full volume like Tevye the Milkman.

Moving beyond the historical argument, Fox sought next to downplay the harm sustained by Lucy Cross and other town residents. No town official coerced Lucy Cross, he stated; she was at liberty to leave the meeting room. Finally, the third judge, Ignatius Restrepo, rose to the challenge.

"A violation of the Establishment Clause does not require coercion, Mr. Fox, does it? Is it not enough for the government to endorse one religion over another? Or is it really your view that the plaintiff would have suffered a constitutional injury only if the town moderator had tied her to her chair?"

"I do respectfully disagree, your Honor," answered Fox, as he buttoned the top button to his suit jacket. "Endorsement may be the standard for addressing the constitutionality of religious displays in public places. But more is required to defeat a publicly held prayer. There must, I submit, be some *element* of coercion before the practice can be declared unconstitutional."

"Element," echoed Judge Restrepo. "But the plaintiff need not be tied to her chair."

"She need not be tied to her chair, no."

"So, what sort of element of coercion would be needed?"

"I suppose," conjectured Fox, "if the town moderator had told Ms. Cross: 'If you leave for the invocation prayer, you cannot come back into the hall to vote.' That's not being tied to a chair, but I would agree it is possibly coercive enough to establish a violation—if the prayer, that is, otherwise met the test for violating the Establishment Clause."

"No doubt that would be sufficient," replied the judge.

"The moderator, of course, never told her any such thing," said Fox. "She was free to come; she was free to leave. And, now on second thought, your Honor, telling her she would not be permitted back in the hall to vote would be a violation of her right to vote, not a violation of the Establishment Clause."

Sam was cranky and tired and feeling ready to bolt, but the courtesies of courtroom protocol kept him tied to his chair.

"Free to come and free to leave," mused Judge Restrepo. "But not to stay. Unless the lady were willing to listen to a prayer she did not want to hear. So not so free in that sense. Why isn't that establishment? It is a prayer arranged and sanctioned by a government official, after all."

"She didn't have to pray. She didn't even have to listen. Your Honor, she could choose to ignore the prayer. She could knit. She could do a Sudoku. Anything at all, within the realm of common courtesy."

"Sudoku, you say? That's Japanese theater, or what?"

"No, no, a puzzle, that's all. She could do a puzzle."

The argument had run its course.

"Thank you, Mr. Fox," said Judge Calabresi. "The court will issue its decision in due course. And, eh, it is not so likely the opinion will be delivered in verse."

Brushing past the salivating press, who were unable to get a statement from them, Sam and Alicia emerged from the courtroom into the marble corridor, joined by Ricky and Sarah. Alicia looked closely at Ricky and pulled him into a hug, and suddenly felt the pressure of tears welling in her eyes as she remembered his turmoil in the court during Gayle Peters's testimony.

He squeezed her back and her tears erupted and rolled down her cheeks, and she buried her face on his shoulder, crying for Kerry and Francine, for Ricky and Clara. Ricky held her, and they all became teary, standing in the hallway in an operatic tableau, while Lionel Fox and a small entourage marched toward them on the marble corridor.

Fox reached into their midst, baffled by the weeping pantomime, to shake Sam's hand. "Nice job," said Fox, and Sam sniffled and returned the compliment.

"I don't know why you cause me so much grief, Ricky," Alicia said as Fox and company departed for the elevators. "It's like you're the son I never had."

"Alicia, I guess I can't say you're the mother I never had. I've got one, but she and you are not alike. I'm glad. I mean I'm glad you're who you are."

Down in Columbus Park, Barb still sat basking in the sunshine, watching the dwindling practitioners of t'ai chi. Her mood had come around. She had removed her fleece and brushed off her negative feelings into the pigeon droppings on the pavement, and when Alicia came to her, she hugged her hard, and then hugged Sam. Surprised to see Sarah and Ricky, she hugged them too, not knowing what to make of their presence.

With her back to the others, Alicia put her hand on Barb's head and she pulled her in close. "Barb, everything all right? You look better, my sweet one." Barb had been in a disgruntled mood when they arrived at Foley Square and had said she needed to sit outside, and there wasn't time to explore the reasons.

"Yes, I am feeling better. I just needed time to sort things out in my head. My stupid head. And this park and this sunshine were perfect. I couldn't handle the court hearing just now. And I made friends with one of those dancers. All right with you, Alicia?"

Alicia nodded and kissed her. Barb held her embrace for a long moment, then said, "I'm glad to see these guys here," tilting her head toward Ricky and Sarah.

For a few minutes, squinting in the brightness, they all talked about the Second Circuit argument and caught up on Sarah's life in Providence, Ricky's new persona as an NYU student, Barb and Alicia's ten-year celebration.

Ricky was uncharacteristically animated. "You won the argument, Sam, no doubt," he said. "You outsmarted the Fox."

"I'm afraid I don't have your youthful confidence," Sam replied. "I really have no idea what the court will do."

"But it's so obviously an establishment of religion."

"You could say that about *Marsh v. Chambers* too, and it gets you nowhere. And remember, a very smart district court judge already held the prayer in Jefferson didn't amount to establishment."

Barb asked, "What's *Marsh v. Chambers*?"

"A Supreme Court case," said Alicia, "where they said it was okay for a state legislature to hold a prayer."

"Judge Wallis was wrong," Ricky said to Sam. "*Marsh* is different, and you explained that really well, Sam. That judge, Calabresi? He's really something. I'm pretty sure he got your points."

"Oh, I know," said Sam. "He got them. He knew them before I said anything. I just don't know if he agrees with them. Judge Rothberger doesn't. And I have no clue about the third guy, Restrepo. It's not looking so good."

"Dad, you're such a pessimist," Sarah said.

"Yeah, okay," he said. "That's me."

"You gave a really solid argument, Sam," said Alicia. "I'm not just saying that because I love you." Sam looked down at his feet, and she added, "I'd say you were brilliant, but I know that would go to your head, so I won't."

"I will," pronounced Sarah. "You *were* brilliant. There, watch his head swell."

"The judges gave Fox just as hard a time as they gave you," said Ricky. He paused and looked up anxiously. "Look, Sam, can I talk to you all about something? Here, come over to the benches." There was a set of benches arranged in a semi-circle near the grass.

It was not clear to Barb whether Ricky intended her to be included, and she held back. But Ricky said, "No, no. Everyone," and gestured for them all to join him on the benches.

Ricky hesitated and glanced around him as if to make sure no one else could hear what he was about to say. "You remember, Sam," Ricky finally announced, "when you asked me about what I wrote to Kerry on Facebook, about her being a lesbian?"

Sam placed his hand along his brow to shield his eyes from the sun and nodded that he remembered.

Ricky spoke quietly now. "I thought maybe I should expose her. I know, I know." He grimaced and shrugged, realizing he didn't need to explain again. "She called me after I sent the first message on Facebook, and was totally upset and crying. I didn't speak to her then; it was just a voice message. I couldn't even understand what she was saying. So, you know, I sent her the second message on Facebook, saying I wanted to meet her at the Sacred Grounds. I wanted to see her and try to talk about it. Her being so freaked out was freaking me out."

All of them were listening. Sam said he remembered all this. "Yeah, Ricky, and you told me you did meet with her, and you decided not to go public with the thing. I have that right?"

"Right, right. We did meet, I told you that. Kerry came to meet me at the café that day. Or the next day actually. She was fiercely worked up, really upset."

Sam noticed the shifting of Ricky's jaw bones as he gritted his teeth, and it brought back a fleeting memory of his running into the kid at the café a year before.

"We talked for over an hour at the Sacred Grounds. She was crying some of the time. Kerry isn't like that at all, normally. She was the sanest kid at school. We were *friends*, did you know?"

Ricky looked for affirmation from the group. "I mean, I really respected her because she was so, like, independent. She never needed to be part of the ridiculous crowd. And I think, well, she even told me, that she respected me, kind of for the same reasons. You know, I always had these strong beliefs and I wasn't afraid to stand up for them. We were the *same* that way. That's the reason she told me she was a lesbian in the first place. She trusted me that much."

He looked down at his feet, and they waited.

Alicia asked him, "So what happened at the café, Ricky?"

On the asphalt court a short distance away, the kids were playing basketball, two elderly men played chess nearby, and the women were dancing their slow t'ai chi dance.

Part V
Hazardous Freedom

"I'll tell you," Ricky said. "Kerry opened up to me, when we were sitting there at the Sacred Grounds. I never told you before because I felt it was so private, and that I owed it to her to keep quiet. I know that sounds inconsistent since I had sort of threatened to out her for being gay. But by then I had decided I wasn't going to do that. I hope you understand."

Alicia nodded. "Perfectly."

"I really got turned around by her. I promised her I wouldn't do it. And then when she told me this other stuff, I said I wouldn't tell anyone."

He paused for a moment, smiling wistfully in the direction of the t'ai chi dancers. "Even after she killed herself, I decided I wasn't going to talk about it. She needed her privacy. Even then, especially then." Again he asked the group, "You understand?"

Everyone was patient. They sat on the benches in the warm sun, waiting for Ricky to continue with his story. A flock of pigeons had arrived, cooing and ducking.

"And then you guys had this case for the principal, Ms. Peters. I wasn't going to screw things up for her, too. So I just kept quiet." He looked around nervously.

"But now, I think I should tell you. You're done with Ms. Peters's case, right?"

Alicia confirmed they were indeed. Neither she nor Sam had ever told Ricky about his mother's fateful email to the other board members.

Ricky looked up at the sky for apparent guidance, working the bones in his jaw again. He sighed heavily. "So Kerry told me she was having a relationship with Ms. Peters. They were, you know, lovers. For like a few months before she died, they were lovers."

A stray basketball bounced in their direction and the flock of pigeons rose as one, and hovered about them, settling back to the ground a moment later.

Barb glanced at Alicia, and realized Alicia had seen this coming, when somehow Barb had not. Barb had worked so closely with Gayle Peters, for so many years. She had thought Gayle was probably gay. But a relationship with a student, a girl of 17? She had no idea. She was suddenly furious at her former very competent boss for being so idiotic, and perhaps furious at herself for not seeing it.

"I go through life with my eyes half-closed, in a state of dream," she muttered. "Fuck, fuck, fuck, fuck," she added.

Alicia shook her head, and pondered how this information would have destroyed the discrimination case she'd argued with such righteousness. Yes, they had uncovered Clara's hateful email proving her discriminatory motive. But the board wouldn't have paid a penny had they known of this bombshell. The principal sleeping with a student! It cannot happen. That much is sacred. All the homophobia in the world couldn't cancel that sin.

Sam was annoyed with the kid he had nurtured for so long. "You *knew*, Ricky? You knew? When Peters was testifying in court, when she made this big revelation that she was a lesbian and had talked with Kerry about it—and I was floundering up there, caught with my pants down—you knew all the time that they were actually having an *affair*?"

"I couldn't tell you about it, Sam." Ricky had raised his voice. "I made a promise to Kerry. Okay? I felt I couldn't tell anyone. I'm sorry. And it wasn't an affair."

"What?" said Sam, irritation rising. "Of course it was."

"Doesn't an affair mean you're cheating on someone? Because Kerry wasn't cheating anyone. And I guess neither was Ms. Peters. Please," said Ricky, "don't make it sound worse."

"Okay, okay," said Sam. "You don't have to cheat to be having an affair. But I don't care what the term is. A relationship, not an affair, whatever we call it. With a minor. It's a crime, for crying out loud. You didn't tell me, and I was trying to represent you."

Ricky had sat there mute during the hearing, all the testimony, the Vietnamese noodle soup, the ride home that night, everything. God damn it. Sam put his head back on the hard bench and closed his eyes to the shining sky.

"I get it, Ricky," he said, "you needed to keep a promise." What a fool I have been, he thought.

Sarah turned to Ricky, wanting to offer comfort. She said, "It figures. Poor Kerry. I bet she thought you already knew about it, Ricky. I mean knew about their relationship, when you sent her the Facebook message? And that's why she was losing it."

"I didn't know about it. You think Kerry thought I knew already?"

Sam stared at his daughter. "Sarah's right! She must be right. I mean this probably explains why Kerry was so distraught." Everybody looked intently at Sam. "It never made sense otherwise, or not enough sense. But when she got your original message on Facebook, she probably thought you knew or had guessed about her relationship with Peters and you were going to make *that* public."

"Oh, shit," said Barb. "Maybe that's it, eh? Kerry didn't care so much about her own exposure. I think I understand it now. She cared about—she was worried about—exposing Gayle. That's the piece that put her over the edge." The last phrase, meant figuratively, clattered in her ears. "I didn't mean it like that. Well, you know what I mean."

"So Kerry was so upset about Ms. *Peters's* reputation?" Ricky looked from one to the other. "Is that really what motivated her? I can't deal with that."

"But I do think that's it," Sam said. "Kerry was smart enough to know the revelation would destroy Peters's career and cause all kinds of legal trouble. So the poor girl was desperate. She wasn't thinking about herself."

Sam closed his eyes, imagining the sensitive teenager Kerry reading Ricky's Facebook threat, imagining her believing that Ricky would go public about her relationship with Gayle Peters, imagining Kerry grasping how the scandal would annihilate her lover's happiness and peace—and imagining Kerry feeling utterly hopeless in all the mess.

"The shame of it all," Sam muttered.

Ricky said, "I didn't know anything about their relationship until that day."

Protective Alicia told him he couldn't have known how Kerry would react. No one could have.

Ricky said to the group, as an afterthought, "I felt terrible for her. She must have been really attracted to Ms. Peters. No, I mean it was more than that. She was in love with her. She told me she couldn't believe her own feelings. But, you know, at the same time Kerry knew the relationship had to end."

He looked up into Alicia's surprised face. "She knew it had to end?"

"Yeah," said Ricky, "Kerry was going to do that. End it. She'd even written a letter she was about to give to Ms. Peters. She showed it to me, at the Sacred Grounds that day."

"A letter?" said Barb Laval. Looking up, she noticed the t'ai chi women were gone. She never saw them leave. Her head ached. She had sat too long in the sun and her head ached. She fished for a pill in her purse, and Alicia silently handed over her water bottle.

"What did it say, Ricky? Do you remember?" Barb asked.

Barb had a vivid recollection of the meeting in Gayle Peters's office with Superintendent Bird and Sergeant LaPorte. LaPorte had showed them a clear plastic bag that held the suicide note in Kerry's handwriting. They had sat around the table and examined it together, a torn piece of paper, with the girl's cursive script, two succinct lines. "I can't go on anymore. I'm sorry." The police officer had told them not to disclose its contents—Gayle Peters had asked about that.

Barb never did reveal any details about the note. Ricky would not have known what was written on it. That was becoming clear to Barb, through the haze of her aching head.

"What did the letter say, Ricky? Can you tell me exactly?"

Ricky tilted his head and tried to answer. "It wasn't much of a letter, really. She had written at the top, Dear Gayle, I remember seeing that. And then she wrote something like, you mean so much to me, or I really care so much about you. She didn't say the word love." He was trying to focus, trying to place himself back in the Sacred Grounds.

"Was there more?" Barb pressed.

"Then below that it said something like she needed to end the relationship, she couldn't keep on seeing Ms. Peters— no, she didn't say Ms. Peters of course. I think she wrote it was all over, or something like that. And I remember it said she was sorry, she used the word sorry. She was ending the relationship." Ricky stopped and looked up at Barb.

The basketball game close by had picked up pace with some older kids, and there was a lot of yelling. The old men continued their chess game. It was just past noon and the park was filling with people bringing cartons of food, wafting aromas of greasy lo mein and oyster sauce.

Barb asked Ricky what kind of paper Kerry's note was on. He didn't know what she meant. "Was it part of a piece of paper, like was it torn or ripped?" she asked him.

"No, it was just a normal piece of paper, I think, white, maybe pulled out of a notebook, the size of a regular notebook, you know, eight by eleven or whatever. I don't remember it being torn."

Sam and Alicia shared a baleful look. Barb drew in a deep shuddering breath, looked around at them all through the gauze of her headache, and told them with passable coherence what she knew and what she thought.

There was no suicide note. There was just a desperate letter by a teenager to end a sexual relationship with a school principal.

It was hotter now, the sun beating on the pavement. Barb wiped her damp forehead and shielded her eyes. "It wasn't a suicide note," she said again.

Alicia stood up and crossed behind the bench where Ricky sat with his legs apart and his bony elbows on his knees. She leaned over him and put her chin on his head, and she spoke softly to him. "Ricky, Kerry didn't jump."

"Kerry didn't jump? It didn't happen? Oh Christ." He drew in his breath sharply, and let it out audibly, his eyes closed. Barb could see in Ricky's face the depth of his sorrow for his friend Kerry. She imagined, hopefully, that she also saw the simultaneous release of his guilt, dandelion seeds dispersing into the breeze.

Ricky tilted his head up to see Alicia. "You mean she murdered her?" he asked.

"I don't know," said Alicia.

Alicia drew Sam aside to the edge of the grass, but Barb could hear them. They conferred about the scope of their ethical obligations of loyalty to a former client. Ricky's revelation of his conversation with Kerry at the café, and Barb's knowledge of Kerry's note—none of this information was given to them by Gayle Peters as a client confidence. They determined they had no obligation to keep it secret.

Alicia pulled her cell phone out of her handbag, got the number for the Montpelier police department off the Internet, and called Sergeant LaPorte. She left a message, asking him if the police had checked Kerry's suicide note for fingerprints, and she'd call him later when she got back to Vermont.

Drawn together by the brutality of their common realization, they joined into a knot of linked arms and worked their way through the crowds of Chinatown and crossed Canal Street into Little Italy. Alicia held on to her vulnerable friend Ricky, and Sarah clasped her father's hand, and they surrounded Barb, who was not in a state to be left to her own devices. They found an open sidewalk table at a restaurant on Mulberry Street.

After a somber lunch, the Vermonters hailed a taxi to JFK to catch their flight home. Ricky and Sarah, though, lingered behind at their sidewalk table, eager to pause together, and too frugal to allow the second bottle of Chianti Classico to go to waste. They sat side by side with their backs to the restaurant window, facing the crowded anonymous street.

The topic of Gayle Peters had exhausted them. Sarah reached over to Ricky, a sweet soul to salve. He'd looked so bewildered, seemed swamped by Kerry's death all over again. She held his hand, to help redirect their conversation. "So," she said, "what courses are you taking this year?" Her father began sentences with the word *so*. Sarah knew she mimicked this verbal tic without wanting to and couldn't seem to stop herself.

Ricky looked at her. He seemed surprised by her interest in him, by the chance to talk about something different. "We can talk about regular life?"

She liked his irony. "Yes, we can, Ricky."

He took her up on it. "The best course is introduction to moral and political philosophy. We've read some John Locke and John Stuart Mill and John Rawls."

"The Johns!" She grinned at him.

Ricky remained serious. "It's really interesting how it fits together," he said as their fingers intertwined. "The readings aren't all by Johns. We read some chapters by this legal philosopher, Ronald Dworkin, who says all the moral concepts are unified. Dworkin taught at NYU before he died last year. I wish I could have heard him."

Sarah said, "I've never read any of that, I'm embarrassed to say." She was also a bit embarrassed about their linked hands. His hand was warm and smooth. She liked the feeling of it.

"Also, I'm taking a required first year English seminar and intro courses in economics and psychology. In psych, the professor is a Freudian, which I guess is strange because they say he's the only one in the department." He asked her, "What kind of stuff do you like to read?"

"Like to? Novels, I suppose, contemporary novels. But I've read a lot of history, like social and cultural history. That's what I studied at Brown. Now I've been reading a lot about Latin America." She told him about her work with Latino migrants in Providence.

Traffic stalled on the street in front of them as a delivery van blocked the road. Men were unloading crates of fruit from the back. Cars honked and people were yelling. The restaurant's *maître d'* appeared and yelled at the men in Italian.

"What do you do for fun?" Ricky asked.

Sarah smiled at this segue. "Not enough."

"Me neither. But I am playing ping pong. That's fun."

"Ping pong?"

"Yup. There's a group in my dorm who plays. It's awesome. Do you play?"

"No, except a bit of fooling around," Sarah answered. All the crates were unloaded, the doors slammed, and the van pulled off. "Oh, but I did read a good book called *Ping-Pong Diplomacy*, about Nixon's détente with China. It began with the American ping pong players being invited to play in China. It's an unbelievable story. One of the U.S. players was a dope-head who wore purple velvet pants."

"No kidding," said Ricky. "I should read it."

"I'll lend you the book. Maybe I could come back to the City and see you and bring the book."

"You'd do that, Sarah?"

"If you'd invite me," she said, smiling. "Or the other way round, you could visit me in Providence."

"Okay," he said. "I think that would be cool. Just for me to borrow the book?" He was teasing her.

Sarah released her hand and said to him, "My dad's always liked you a lot. You know?"

"I think I do know. I am so lucky, Sarah."

"You mean lucky that my dad likes you? It's not luck, Ricky. It's because you're the person you are. He has a lot of respect for you. He's told me that a number of times."

The driver of a motor scooter pulled his bike up on the sidewalk near them and was removing his helmet. "He kind of thinks you have a heart of gold," Sarah told Ricky as she watched the events on the sidewalk. The *maître d'* emerged again and yelled again, this time in English. The biker swore at him in Italian and pulled off.

"I didn't understand what he was talking about before." She smiled broadly at Ricky. "But now I think I do."

Ricky listened with embarrassment and remained silent and Sarah continued. "My dad drives me a bit crazy sometimes.

I suppose that's a parent-child thing. When I left home for college, I pulled away from my parents and wasn't in touch very much. I guess my father liked to be a mentor to a teenager. I was gone and there you were. A perfect mentee."

"So you're taking credit?" said Ricky. "Well, then, thank you."

They watched a group of Wall Street types congregate near them, trying to decide whether to eat at this restaurant or another. The group decided on another and crossed the street.

"Why does Sam drive you crazy?" Ricky asked her.

"Oh, you know," she said. "Don't your parents do that to you? My dad is big, not in a threatening way, but his presence, his voice, it saturates the air and occupies the space around him and I felt sometimes that I wasn't free to be myself. He's like the old growth tree in the forest. This sounds trite and I hate trite. But it's true, and then I overreact by being too assertive and critical." She shrugged. "By being childish, maybe. Which perpetuates the problem. It just makes him bigger."

They sat again in silence amidst the noise of the street. Ricky said, "My experience with your father is kind of the opposite. His mind didn't oppress me. It freed me."

He looked over at Sarah and held her in his gaze for several seconds. Sarah was astonished by Ricky's intensity, and she felt responsible not to let him down, like she was holding his heart in her hands. She felt a brush of euphoria.

But Sarah could not give voice to such a feeling, so she teased instead: "So, are you hitting on me here?" Even though she was the one who had hit first.

Ricky blushed. "Um, I don't know. Is that what I'm doing? It's an awful expression."

The waiter came out and addressed Ricky. "Anything else, sir? Dessert perhaps? A coffee, cappuccino? For the signorina?"

Ricky, unused to being addressed as *sir*, looked at Sarah for confirmation and said, "No, thank you. We're all set."

The bill had been paid already by the others, now on their way to Vermont. The waiter removed the empty wine bottle and left.

The momentary magic was gone and the noise of the traffic intruded. "I can't get it out of my head," said Ricky. "Principal Peters. Do *you* think she killed Kerry? Pushed her off the cliff?"

"I don't know," she said. "It's hard to imagine. I don't want to think about it. Maybe I don't even want to know the truth about that. Maybe I would rather live with the uncertainty." She looked at Ricky and added, "I'm sorry."

"No reason for you to be sorry, Sarah. There probably is no clear way to get at the truth anyway. I wouldn't trust whatever Peters has to say about it." He looked down at his bony knees. "But somehow I do want to know what the truth is. Should I tell you if I find out?"

He was serious and this amused Sarah. She didn't know what to answer and just blushed and smiled at him. Ricky waited a moment and then said, "I never imagined I'd be sitting here like this with you. I mean, I had no idea you would be here at all. But I'm talking about beyond that. This whole thing." He swept his arm around. "Here, us."

"Me too," she said. "I like it."

Where the overwhelming predominance of prayers offered are associated, often in an explicitly sectarian way, with a particular creed, and where the town takes no steps to avoid the identification, but rather conveys the impression that town officials themselves identify with the sectarian prayers and that residents in attendance are expected to participate in them, a reasonable objective observer would perceive such an affiliation.

Galloway v. Town of Greece, 681 F.3d 20, 34 (2d
Cir. 2012) (Calabresi, J.) (involving challenge to
prayer practice at town government *board meetings*),
reversed by U.S. Supreme Court, 82 U.S.L.W. 4334
(5/5/14)

In Montpelier, in its glory of October foliage, the police
gathered evidence and conferred with the prosecutors.
Meanwhile, Sam Jacobson brooded in his office, unable to
concentrate on work. He wandered into Alicia's office and sat
down, saying nothing.

"You're letting all this get you down," she offered.

"All this?"

"Gayle Peters and Kerry Pearson."

"Yeah, it's getting me down. What a mess, Alicia. I misjudged
it all."

"Sam, who didn't? The good thing is Ricky is relieved. I
mean, you could see it on his face."

"I don't know, Alicia. Maybe so, but it doesn't change the
horrible facts, whatever the fuck the facts are. I should quit the
practice."

"Well, there's a *non* sequitur, Sam. You threaten to do that,
I'll quit first and leave you all alone," she said with a big smile,
knowing none of it would come to pass.

But he wouldn't allow her to humor him, and continued
in the same vein. "I'm not sure I can do it anymore. I've been
thinking about the Second Circuit argument too. I know I've let
Lucy Cross down. I think we'll get a bad decision. They'll say
something like prayer at town meeting is just a solemn ritual,
nothing inherently religious. We'll lose."

"Sam, you don't know that. Are you like this at home?"

"Like what?"

"A sourpuss?"

"No, never. You feel like going for lunch?"

"Let me take you out, Sam. How about the Pound Silver Taproom? Let's get a burger and onion rings and a glass of beer."

"I'm sorry I'm a sourpuss, Alicia. Let me get my jacket, and let's go."

The next day, two weeks to the day after the oral argument in *Lucy Cross v. Town of Jefferson*, the Second Circuit decision arrived by email. Sam read the bottom line first. "Reversed," it said.

"Reversed!" he yelled. Lucy Cross had won her appeal. He then read it from the top. It was a victory, but a qualified victory.

Judge Calabresi, in a unanimous opinion, wrote that the proper inquiry was "whether the town's practice, viewed in its totality by an ordinary, reasonable observer, conveyed the view that the town favored or disfavored certain religious beliefs." Sam wondered sardonically who in Jefferson Center might be considered ordinary or reasonable.

The inquiry, opined Calabresi, was "fact-intensive" and "case-specific." These hyphenated adjectives camouflaged an admission of the court's inability to articulate a concise legal rule that could be broadly applied.

"On the record before us," the opinion went on, "the town's prayer practice must be viewed as an endorsement of a particular religious viewpoint." Although reluctant to "parse" the content of the prayers, the court recognized what could not possibly be denied, that "most of the prayers at issue here contained uniquely Christian references."

And it was this "steady drumbeat" of sectarian Christian prayers, as Calabresi wrote with more drama than usual, that inevitably affiliated the town with Christianity, in violation of "the clear command of the Establishment Clause."

So what qualified the victory? "We emphasize what we do

not hold," wrote the judge. "We do not hold that the town may not open its public meetings with a prayer or invocation." *Marsh* precluded that. This meant the court rejected *Lee v. Weisman*, the school graduation prayer case, as the relevant precedent, and also ignored Sam's attempt to distinguish the rights of voting citizens from the duties of legislators.

"Nor do we hold that any prayers offered in this context must be blandly nonsectarian. Occasional prayers recognizing the divinities or beliefs of a particular creed, in a context that makes clear that the town is not endorsing or affiliating itself with that creed or, more broadly, with religion or nonreligion, are not offensive to the Constitution."

Sam reflected back on Judge Calabresi's questions during the oral argument. An ecumenical, rotational system would be permitted. A minister, an imam, and *kumbaya*.

But Sam could hear Lucy Cross beaming with pleasure when she heard the news from him on the phone. "This is a gift from God!" she told Sam. He explained the limitations of the court's ruling.

"If we have to rotate among the deities, I can live with that," she said. "Not that I'll be around too much longer to see a lot of rotation. I might just rotate out of this earthy world. But don't you worry about that, Sam. Right now, I feel blessed."

"That's good to hear, Lucy."

"Do you, Sam? Do you feel blessed?"

"No," he answered. "I have never felt blessed. I have too much angst."

In truth, neither she nor Sam believed the attitudes of her Jefferson Center neighbors toward her would change one whit for the better. Not in the short run. The court ruling might just harden them. Now they would hate judges too. *Activist* judges, as Fox News called them.

A lawyer who has formerly represented a client in a matter . . . shall not thereafter . . . use information relating to the representation to the disadvantage of the former client. . .

Vermont Rules of Professional Conduct [for Attorneys] 1.9(c)

The weather was turning cold again; the wind had picked up, stripping the trees of their leaves. The tourists had come in buses for foliage season, spent their flatlander money on maple syrup, scenic Vermont calendars, and local crafts, and were gone. Days were getting depressingly shorter again. A confidential criminal investigation of a high school principal was nearing completion.

Alicia Santana and Sam Jacobson were in their Chamber Street office, in the lavender dusk of afternoon, waiting for the arrival of Gayle Peters. Gayle herself was planning on leaving Vermont in a couple of weeks, for North Carolina. She would stay with her sister and her husband, who owned an electrical supply company, and had a spare bedroom. Gayle had earlier shown Alicia her sister's letter assuring her of a place "as long as you like while you sort yourself out."

Peters had not been told the purpose of this meeting with the lawyers and probably assumed it was concerned with loose ends from her lawsuit. In fact, she was about to be ambushed.

They stood in the conference room with the large windows overlooking the busy street below. They watched a group of backpack-laden high school students heading home, jostling and flirting. They saw Gayle walking from the direction of Sproul Street and crossing Chamber; she disappeared from view and, in a moment, they heard the bell chime.

"Come in, come in." Sam was the designated speaker. "Gayle," he said, as they shook hands, "I hope you are doing all right," a statement that sounded ridiculous and cruel to his own ears.

Gayle replied, "Fine, fine, sort of. How are you both?" She cast them a quizzical look. Alicia had been her attorney, not Sam.

"Coffee? Water?" Sam asked. She declined and sat down.

"We asked you here for this meeting," Sam proceeded, "to advise you of some new information. As you know, the firm's representation of you, in your discrimination case against the school, concluded several months ago, once your final settlement was negotiated and executed. So we are not now considering you a client, but only wish to share some new information, as I said. Okay?"

"Okay." Guarded.

"And of course, we did not represent you in connection with Ricky Stillwell's suit against the school district."

Peters looked at him with puzzlement and said nothing. Alicia looked at him too, thinking the preamble was too long and too formal. C'mon Sam, her eyes said, cut to the chase.

"We had a discussion, Alicia and I, with Ricky Stillwell. We saw him in New York recently. Gayle"—he cleared his throat—"Ricky told us that he met with Kerry Pearson at the Sacred Grounds Café last November, right after he sent her that Facebook message. At that time, Kerry shared some personal information with him."

Gayle Peters was facing them in her expensive clothes, sitting erect in her chair, the white streak in her hair commanding attention. But her eyes looked exceedingly weary. Again, she didn't speak, and waited for Sam to continue.

"I'll just come out and be frank with you, Gayle. Kerry told Ricky at the café that day about her relationship with you, her sexual relationship with you."

Gayle gritted her teeth and froze. Could she survive this revelation? These were her attorneys; they would not make this public, surely. Should she deny it? Maybe this wouldn't change anything. Her mind raced. Alicia could see it, but then Sam kept on talking.

"Ricky also told us," said Sam, "that Kerry was prepared to end the relationship with you. She showed him a letter, a note. He told us what Kerry had written on the note."

Sam again cleared his throat, for no good reason except nervousness. "Ricky said the note was about Kerry Pearson ending her relationship with you. She was going to give you the note telling you the relationship was over."

He paused to let Gayle absorb these words. Her face was ashen.

"Gayle, now I need to tell you something about this note Kerry was going to give you, to end the relationship with you. It was the same type of paper, with the same words, as Kerry's supposed suicide note. This could not be a coincidence." He paused again, cleared his throat again. "The police tested the paper for fingerprints. And, well, you know whose prints were on it. They found your prints on the note that was found with Kerry's body."

Now Gayle broke. She knew they knew; she saw it all. "I loved that girl," she muttered. "I didn't mean to. She was all my happiness, and she was ending it. She fell. She *fell*."

After a moment's hesitation, she spoke again in a hoarse voice. "She loved me too. She wasn't a kid. I didn't take advantage, you know," she added absurdly.

Alicia couldn't hold back. "You didn't take advantage?" Then she thought better of her approach. "How did you do it?" she asked. "I mean, the relationship. Where would you go?"

Gayle stared at her with annoyance. And as she spoke again, the note of defiance returned. "Sometimes we'd be in my office in the evening. What do you think? Or we'd go to my place. Perfectly discreet. It started in the summer, so the school was basically vacant. Other places, too. There was really no harm."

"And you went to Mahady Park?" suggested Sam, hand stroking his chin.

"Yes. We sometimes took walks up there in the dark. We were so secretive about everything, even in spring after lacrosse practices, before we were . . . well, before. Nobody knew, and we could have kept it that way. There was no harm."

She stopped.

Sam prodded. "Except Kerry decided to end the relationship."

"Yes, Sam. Kerry wanted to end it."

"Tell us what happened, Gayle."

Elegant Gayle crumpled some more. "We were walking. We were on the trail at the crest of that big outcrop. We were arguing, not loudly; we were quiet about everything. She had given me that note earlier in the evening. At my office. The custodians were off that evening, and I would just lock the outside door so no one could come in. We had even drunk a bottle of wine together in my office, and I wanted to . . . I wanted to be with her. But she wasn't into it. We were a bit drunk. I guess that was risky, come to think of it."

Ya think? Alicia almost said, but didn't as Sam cast her a warning look, and Gayle rolled on. "Something else was going on with her, and we talked, and then she gave me that letter. And then for some reason we headed out and drove to Mahady Park. I'm not really sure why we did that. Except that was a place we went. We'd often go there to talk. I told you that. We could walk and nobody was there at night. Not in November."

"And?"

"I was afraid, you know, terrified about being left behind. Imagine, Alicia, if Barb walked out on you." The comparison, of course, was absurd and offended Alicia, but she kept quiet. "I should have just walked away." Here Gayle paused and studied her hands on her lap. "Yes, I should have walked away, but I didn't. I needed her. And then, we were arguing, like I said.

"Somehow we moved off the trail closer to the edge—stupid, and she grabbed me. Why did she grab me like that? Just at that place at that moment? She went off the edge. By accident! She was drunk, you understand? She yanked and I swung her away from me. I didn't mean to. I was crazy. I didn't think it would kill her. I ran down the trail, around to the bottom."

Sam asked, "And what happened next?" Soft voice.

"She must have broken her neck. I don't know. It was awful. I was desperate. What could I do? So I had a crazy idea. I saw the note could be read in a different way if some words were missing. I tore it carefully, tore off edges to cut off some of the words. No one was there. I had this penlight on my car keys, so I could see what I was doing. It looked like a suicide note, didn't it? So of course there was her handbag and I put the note inside it. Why not?"

Sam and Alicia were not inclined to answer, and waited. Gayle said: "And then later, well, later I found out about the sick thing Ricky Stillwell put on Facebook about Kerry. And the whole story made more sense. She had a reason to commit suicide, you see. What was the harm?"

A door from the conference room led to Alicia's office. It opened and Sergeant Barry LaPorte emerged, looking grimmer than he usually did. He tucked a digital recorder into his jacket pocket. "Hello all," he said to the room in general, and then to Gayle: "You're coming with me now."

Peters said, "Oh God. You fucked me over."

LaPorte looked at Sam briefly and nodded. "Nice with the fingerprints."

Peters barked, "What do you mean?"

Sam didn't know LaPorte well, so he was surprised when the cop replied to Gayle without rancor or even curtness, but with courtesy. "Fair question. We'll talk about it on our way in my cruiser. I'll read you your rights. Let's not use cuffs, all right?"

❧

Again, Alicia and Sam stood by the office window looking out, street lights glowing in the cold twilight. They saw Barry LaPorte escort Gayle Peters from the building. The room was blissfully quiet and their eyes met. "You done good, Sam," she whispered, in the sort of frontier grammar weirdly appropriate to the moment.

"Not really. I missed everything." After a few moments, he asked, "Why didn't Ricky tell us in the beginning?"

"You know him better than I do, Sam."

"He was trying to protect Kerry," Sam offered. "His devotion to her, to her privacy, and her trust and friendship, all of that overcame his religious zeal. He did the right thing. Don't you think? In the end, he did the right thing?"

"Yes, he did."

"So he did act out of love."

"He did act out of love, Sam. Outstanding kid. A little naïve." They looked steadily at each other. "As for Gayle and Kerry Pearson," she said, "I guess that was a kind of love too. Free love. But talk about hazardous freedom. . . . That phrase from *Tinker*," she explained.

"I wouldn't honor it with the name *love*," he said. "It's exploitation."

"Yeah, maybe, but I'm gathering that Kerry's feelings were real—Gayle's too, fucked up as that is. I think the woman was afraid of an adult relationship, afraid an adult would see all her warts and blemishes. So she needed a girl to be in love with."

"Look at the context," Sam said. "She's the principal, Kerry's the student. It's inherently unequal."

Alicia nodded. "No doubt," she said. "You know, I think it happens a lot."

Sam shook his head.

"You don't believe me? People in authority, and it's usually men, falling in love, or imagining that's what they're doing, and taking advantage of subordinates—"

He interrupted, "We're talking about a high school principal here. A special case."

"Still, it happens," Alicia insisted.

"You're not condoning it, are you?"

"No, I'm just saying it doesn't surprise me."

"I can't say that, but I will say I never trusted her," he said.

"Because?"

"Don't you ever make judgments about people?"

"Rarely," she answered.

Sam excused himself and called Donna. "How did it go? Are you all right?" she asked.

"No," he said. "I feel like shit. It went fine. She admitted she was with Kerry that night in the park. She says Kerry's fall was kind of an accident though. I suppose she told us the truth, or at least some truth. But I bet it wasn't the whole truth."

"Stay there, Sam. I can get off. I'm coming over. Give me twenty minutes."

Alicia too was on the phone, with Barb, who was waiting at the high school. Then she called Francine Loughlin.

Francine already knew from Barry what had been planned for that afternoon. "Oh Frannie, are you ready to hear this?" Alicia was on the edge of tears.

Barb Laval arrived at the office while Alicia finished her call with Francine. The story was told again. "I worked with the woman for ten years," Barb said. "It's unbelievable. But I guess fingerprints don't lie."

"Actually," said Alicia, "we made that up. The police couldn't get any usable prints off the notepaper."

"You trickster!" said Barb.

When Donna arrived, Barb and Alicia were already on their way downstairs, arm in arm, heading to their old farmhouse across from the red barn.

Donna greeted them at the street-side doorway, came up to the office, and fixed her calm blue-grey eyes on her husband.

The following spring, as classes and exams wrapped up, Ricky decided he was ready for a trip home to Montpelier. He called Sarah Jacobson in Providence. "Will you come with me?" he asked. "I could use your company."

Sarah was happy to hear this. Since that day at the courthouse and Columbus Park in New York, she and Ricky found themselves engaged in what he called a "courtship." He told her he liked the old-fashioned sound of the word.

She saw him briefly in late October when she came to New York for meetings with an immigrant rights group, squeezing in lunch with Ricky during an hour's interval. It was rushed and unsatisfying, but there was enough promise in the encounter to inspire Ricky to write a letter to Sarah, delivered the slow way, with a stamp.

"I want you to know a couple of things," he wrote. "One is I believe in God and I want you to respect that. I think you don't believe in God, and this is something we should talk more about. The other is that I don't believe anymore that homosexuality is wrong. I think you know that already about me, but I want it in writing like this. It doesn't seem like people really have a choice about that, they just are who they are. And even if they do have a choice about it, so what? I am confessing to you, Sarah. I did something awful and inexcusable when I wrote the message to Kerry."

Sarah carried that letter with her for days.

"Dear Ricky," she wrote back in time. "I don't think you have to worry so much about these things. It's true, I don't believe in God. I also don't really understand what you mean when you say you do, and I do want to talk about it with you. I want to learn more about your beliefs. On the other topic, I know you feel dejected about what happened with Kerry. I am not sure it is 'inexcusable' as you say. There are parts of my past I wish I could do over, when I get in a certain mood. I doubt that is very useful. The best we can do is to say, yeah, I did that, I take responsibility, I have learned, and I go forward as a better person. I would like to see you very soon. How about it?"

The first time Ricky came to see Sarah in Providence, she asked him to stay at her apartment. There was the one bed.

They were getting along so well, conversing easily, eating a vegetarian lasagna Sarah had made, drinking beer, laughing at parental eccentricities. They cleaned the dishes, side by side at the sink. Sarah turned toward him, held his right hand with her left, and placed her other hand, wet and sudsy, on the middle of his chest. "Ricky," she said, smiling into his eyes. "What do you think?"

Ricky didn't quite know. He did feel desire, and, yes, he thought, love. He was most uncertain and shy about the prospects relating to the one bed.

"Um, Sarah," he said. "You know, well maybe you don't know. I haven't done this before."

"That shouldn't be a problem," said Sarah, thinking she knew what he meant, and leaned in and up to kiss him on the lips. Full and square, opening his mouth, tongues touching.

When he eventually pulled back, he told her, "Sarah, I don't have a clue what I'm doing."

"I suppose I don't have a clue either, in this precise situation." She brushed the wet area of his shirt.

"But like, more generally you do. Have a clue."

She looked up into his eyes, moist with emotion. Perhaps she had more experience than Ricky, but she was the one who trembled. "I just know this feels totally right. I am very hungry for you."

"I'm developing an appetite too," he said. He took her hand in a burst of uncharacteristic confidence and placed it over the front of his pants. "You can see what I mean," he said.

They took turns in the bathroom. Sarah lit candles, perhaps motivated by some romantic instinct, though she was not at all in the habit of lighting candles. When he sat beside her on the edge of the bed, she asked carefully, "Does your God permit this?"

"What, the candles?"

They grinned like fools at each other.

It was not all straightforward. Ricky's shirt tail got badly stuck in the zipper of his pants, something that had never happened to him before.

"Let me help you," offered Sarah, and she knelt down before him where he sat on the edge of the bed. She worked to extract the shirt from the zipper and as she did so she felt his erection pushing up and this made the problem more difficult. After a few moments of struggle, she was successful with the zipper and then it seemed to Sarah that it just made good sense to help Ricky resolve the erection problem as well. She used her hands and her mouth to do this, and concentrated all her efforts. Ricky lay back gasping in wonderment, and finally screamed in the moment of his ejaculation.

Sarah lurched up. "Ricky! Are you all right?"

"Yes, I think so," he whispered, and he clutched onto her. "I'm just embarrassed."

"But no guilt?"

"Nothing like that."

"Oh, sweet Ricky." She pulled off his pants and his socks and underwear. He removed his shirt and T-shirt, and watched her closely as she removed her own clothing. They climbed under the sheets.

He had never had an ejaculation before. He told her. "Sarah, I mean, you know, I've never even masturbated or anything. It wasn't part of my life. I'm in a foreign land here."

"All right," she said. "Can I ask—?"

"You can ask anything." Ricky noticed again her open and fresh face, a breath of springtime.

"Is it how you expected?"

"Expected?" He laughed. "There were no expectations. It is otherworldly. I don't even know if it will be similar next time. Do you?"

"Oh, sweet Ricky. How would I know?" She pulled him in to a deep kiss, and he tasted his mysterious self in her saliva, and his hand found her breast and hard nipple. That is how their sexual congress began.

Later, once things had quieted down, Sarah reached to the wooden crate she used as a shelf next to the bed and grabbed a book. "Here it is, Ricky, *Ping-Pong Diplomacy*. Like Nixon and China, we are now in full détente."

"Détente means being naked together? Then I guess we are. But the image of Nixon and Mao together in the buff is a definite turn-off. Easier to imagine Putin naked, on a horse." He thought for a moment. "I'm sure you didn't care at all for me before, when I wrote the stuff to Kerry Pearson and all that. Is that all now behind us? Is that why we're in détente?"

"The truth is," she said, "I didn't really know you. It was all old family stories, and then I heard about the incident with Kerry, and so, yeah, I made judgments. They were too hasty. And now I've gotten to know you, and you have changed your views too. As for détente," she said, "would you please come back on top of me now," and he did.

Ricky came again to Providence two weeks later, and stayed for three nights. Then Sarah visited him at NYU, staying with him in his dorm room, and they took meandering walks through Greenwich Village, glued to each other. The glue had held for another week-long visit back in Providence.

"Of course," she told him now on the phone. "We'll go up to Montpelier together. When?"

An interview with Government agents in a situation such as the one shown by this record simply does not present the elements which the Miranda court found so inherently coercive as to require its holding. Although the "focus" of an investigation may indeed have been on Beckwith at the time of the interview in the sense that it was his tax liability which was under scrutiny, he hardly found himself in the custodial situation described by the Miranda Court as the basis for its holding.

Beckwith v. United States, 425 U.S. 341, 347 (1976)

On the Friday in mid-May when the lovers drove north in her friend William's Toyota with the bad muffler and missing front passenger window, the lilacs and crab apples of the Vermont countryside ablaze like their feelings, the defeated Gayle Peters was being sentenced in criminal court over in Gibson Falls.

After an initial skirmish over whether her admissions should be suppressed because they were obtained using trickery—a motion the judge had denied because Peters was neither in custody at the time of her meeting at the lawyers' office nor had she yet been formally charged—Peters had entered a plea to involuntary manslaughter in exchange for the State dismissing charges of murder and statutory rape (under the section of the rape law that prohibits even consensual sex with a child of sixteen to seventeen years old who "is entrusted to the actor's care by authority of law").

Alicia Santana went to court for the sentencing. In the hallway before things got started, she ran into Sergeant LaPorte. "How is she doing, Barry?" Alicia asked.

"Frannie? Much better," he said. "Much better. She's been working part-time back at the office. And sleeping through the night. It's a haul, but much better. Thank you, Alicia. She's not coming here for this thing. She wouldn't stomach it."

As they entered the courtroom, he added, "Come see us, Alicia. You and Barb both. Frannie would like that."

"Oh Barry, I'm so glad to hear these things. You have been amazing. I mean it. I'm so grateful."

"Nonsense," he said, smiling nonetheless. "How are things with you?"

"Good, except for all of this."

Clara Stillwell was also present in the courtroom for the sentencing hearing, and she looked askance at Alicia, who tried a friendly greeting. Gayle Peters's back was to them both, which was a mercy.

Alicia sat down on a bench near the back, next to a man of about her age. He was unshaven and grim. Alicia nodded to him. Looking closely at her face, he said, "You're one of the lawyers, aren't you? You represented that woman." He gestured toward Peters.

"Well yes, in another case, nothing to do with this criminal case. Alicia Santana," she said, holding out her hand, smiling.

He shook her hand. "I thought so. I saw your picture in the paper. I'm Caleb Salt." He leaned toward Alicia and said conspiratorially, "I'm the one who found the girl. Me and my dog, walking in Mahady Park that morning. I couldn't sleep for days."

"How horrible," said Alicia.

The judge was announced and they stood.

As part of the plea deal, the State had agreed not to advocate for a sentence of more than five years' imprisonment. But the judge was not similarly constrained. He asked Peters what she wished to offer in mitigation. Peters spoke to the judge of her horror at what she had done. The judge heard her out, and gave her a lecture and six years. Too little, thought Clara Stillwell. Too long, thought Alicia Santana. Time would be served in a prison in North Carolina because of the shortage of beds in Vermont's sole prison for women. Peters got her wish to move to North Carolina.

Alicia and Caleb Salt started for the door. "What does it mean?" he asked her.

Alicia said, "I think she'll serve most of that time in prison. She may get let out early for good behavior."

"Good behavior!" said Caleb Salt, and he snorted. "Too late for that."

Sam was not present at this hearing, in part because he and Donna were attending a funeral at the United Church on the Jefferson Center town green. Lucy Cross had completed her full rotation and taken her exit.

The service was well attended. Everyone there professed admiration for Lucy's spirited determination, and a few offered sideways tributes to her cantankerousness. "Lucy kept us on our toes with all her views on things, yuh." "She liked to shake things up, that's for sure." "I don't know what kind of demons drove that Lucy Cross sometimes." The service was secular.

Meanwhile, Ricky and Sarah drove noisily across the Scape River into Montpelier. "Ricky," Sarah said. "I'm wondering if you'll do something with me. We have some time. Could we go up to Mahady Park first? Will you show me the place where it happened?"

They parked the old car in a small gravel lot at one of the several park entrances on the north side of town, off of Smiley Street, and walked up the steep path. In twenty minutes they arrived at the place at the bottom of the outcrop. This was the fourth time he had visited the spot since Kerry's death, he told her.

They stood silently. Remnants of flowers and a few odd objects—a stuffed bear, a lacrosse stick, a bracelet—were perched on a stretch of rock ledge to honor Kerry's memory. In his head Ricky recited a prayer and Sarah watched him.

Ricky took Sarah's hand and led her on the trail that wound up and around and eventually came to the top of the cliff. The new foliage mostly blocked the view. On the dry grassy mound a half dozen yards from the verge, they lay down in the dappled sunlight, with their shoes kicked off, his lanky body next to hers. He was quiet, and Sarah let him be.

He noticed the scent of her skin warmed by their trek up the trail. It intoxicated him and he breathed it in. She fell asleep with her head resting on Ricky's arm, her brown hair cut short now, the curls gone.

"We have a strange history," she said when she awoke suddenly. "How did we get here?"

"We climbed up the trail. Beyond that, I have no idea," he replied. "There are so many mysteries. The greatest mystery is you being interested in me. I'm a kid and you're way older and more mature and more worldly. I can't make any sense of it."

She was frowning.

"Are you okay?" he asked her. "You seem troubled."

"Yes, okay," she said. "I had a dream, that's all. But it's gone now. It was something about Kerry. And a canoe trip, I think. Kerry was in the car with us, and it became a boat, and she was urging us upstream, against the current. And the boat became a canoe and we were struggling in the rapids and suddenly Kerry was swept over the edge into the roiling water. The canoe spun around in the light, the dappled light, and I opened my eyes and you were looking into them. But stop already with this more worldly business."

"Well, it's true," he said, and she didn't need to pursue it.

Ricky sat up and crossed his bony legs. "Kerry really did go on canoe trips, you know? I remember once we ran into each other. I was kayaking on my own on the Scape near Gibson Falls, where it runs a little deeper, that's where I'd put in, and Kerry and her friend Sophie were there with a canoe. I like came around a bend, and there they were, stopped on a sand bar. They were next to the canoe reading books in the sun, so I stopped too and we hung out. Kerry had just come back from Italy where she had gone with her mom and she was pretty high about that."

Sarah too sat up, facing Ricky.

"Sarah, listen, it was then—in the river?—that Kerry told me she was a lesbian. I didn't know anything about that until then. I'm not sure why she told me. Maybe it was sort of a challenge. But she wanted me to know and she felt good about it. That was pretty clear. Sophie already knew, of course. Sophie wasn't like that; she had a boyfriend then. Well, maybe that has nothing to do with it at all, what the heck do I know?"

"So how did it make you feel?" asked Sarah.

"At the time? Then? Maybe uncomfortable at first. I really didn't know much. I had no experience. As you know very well." He looked at her for a reaction, but she just continued to watch him with interest.

"Maybe she didn't either," Ricky went on. "I don't know. But she knew that much about herself. And she had enough confidence to tell me, although she probably knew enough about me at the time to realize I would judge her. But there was something about being on a sandbar in the middle of the

Scape with the water flowing all around us that freed us. I really didn't judge her at the time. I just took it in, kind of mystified. It was quite a bit later, maybe a year or more, that I began to feel there was something terribly wrong with the idea. And then eventually I felt I had to do something about it. But, Sarah, thinking back on it now, I admire her."

"Me too," said Sarah. "I admire her too."

"You want to know what book she was reading? It was a collection of poems that had been translated from the Cree language. I remember because she read some of the poems out loud to us. Magical poems about animals like bears playing tricks on the author. The river was gurgling all around us as she was reading. We were sitting there on the sandbar with our feet in the water, and Kerry read these poems, and I suppose they were about spirits interfering with people's lives, and the whole scene seemed in harmony. You know what I mean? I was happy, Sarah."

For a couple of minutes they sat quietly and listened to the light wind playing in the leaves.

He said, "It is time for me to go. All right? Let's walk down."

They walked back to the car and Sarah got in. "I hope this goes well, Ricky," she said through the open window. "I'll see you later, my sweet friend, at the Jacobson manor."

With her daughter's imminent trip home, Donna had planned a dinner party at the house that Friday evening. "Of course, bring Ricky," she had told Sarah on the phone the week before. "Dad will love this. I'll see if the Stillwells can come. We'll invite Alicia and Barb too. They wouldn't miss it."

"Should be a hoot," Sarah had said. "Especially if Clara and Dad start talking about religion. But really, Mom, you guys are still friends with Clara, after Dad and Alicia represented Peters and all that?"

"I think so. I think enough time has passed. Clara should have forgiven Sam his trespasses by now. We have a long history and that means a lot to me, and to them. And if Ricky's coming, it just makes it all more complete."

Then Lucy Cross died and the funeral was scheduled on Friday, the same day as Sarah's arrival. But changing the date for the party wouldn't work because Alicia and Barb had long-time plans for a Montreal excursion on the weekend, where, miracle of miracles, they had agreed to attempt a rapprochement with Barb's old dad, who was maneuvering painfully into 21st-century morality. The dinner party, still scheduled for Friday evening, became a potluck.

Ricky now stood outside the yellow house on Baker Street, wondering how he was going to say what he wanted to say. He walked up onto the porch and pressed the door bell. Francine opened the door. "Hi, Ms. Loughlin. I'm Ricky Stillwell."

He had not called or written in advance, though Sarah had urged him to. Yet Francine did not seem surprised. She held the door and looked him up and down with a gentle expression. "Hello Ricky," she said. "Would you like a drink of something, iced tea perhaps? We can sit out here on the porch."

They sat on the rocking chairs with tall glasses of iced tea. The warm spring air moved through the new green unfurling leaves of the maples in the yard. The lilacs in full bloom surrounded the porch.

With occasional glances up to meet her eyes, Ricky, red with contrition, spoke to Francine of his sorrow, of his friendship with Kerry, and his admiration for her, of his once-held views on homosexuality, and his disavowal, of their fateful conversation at the coffeehouse, of his mortification, of the infamy of Gayle Peters, of his regrets. Francine held her peace while he spoke.

"I beg you," Ricky concluded, "I beg you, Ms. Loughlin, for your forgiveness."

Francine rested her head back on the rocking chair. Her eyes became misty and she closed them. The sun poured in the porch, glancing off Francine's burnt orange hair, the color of baked sweet potato. "Okay, Mr. Stillwell," she said at long last. "Or maybe I'll call you Ricky if you call me Francine."

She opened one eye and he nodded. "You don't need forgiveness, but as you asked for it, I'll give it. You did only one thing I can object to. Then you changed course immediately. And after that, Ricky Stillwell, you did everything well. That's pretty good, for a teenager. I never held you responsible for what happened. Certainly not now."

Ricky gazed at her, gauging her sincerity. "Really?" he whispered. "Thank you, Francine."

They both sat quietly on the porch. "Kerry and I went to Italy a couple of years ago," Francine began again. "We stayed in a village called Vernazza on the coast. It's a beautiful old fishing village. We hiked on the trails in the hillsides around the village, amid lemon trees and vineyards and olive groves. One morning we met up with an Australian couple, I guess in their seventies. We walked together in the morning, and had lunch with them at a little restaurant in one of the neighboring villages, fresh fish and local white wine.

"Both Kerry and I somehow hit it off with this couple. We sat outside on the restaurant terrace, overlooking the sea. We got up to leave, and the gentleman stood up and fell over. He had a heart attack, right there. He was lying on his back on the terrace, looking straight up at his wife. He said to her, *This is it, my dear. I am happy. Very happy. No worries. Carry on.* And he died. It was that sudden.

"I can hear his voice now as I tell it to you. We stayed with the lady of course, and there were all kinds of discussions across language barriers with the restaurant owner and then local police and doctors and various officials. We stayed with her throughout the day and evening. Her name was Marjorie. Kerry had questions and wasn't too shy. You probably know that, Ricky. She asked Marjorie whether her husband was really happy, as he had said. *Oh yes, I think he was*, Marjorie explained. *Because he knew love*."

Francine stopped there, and when Ricky looked over at her, her eyes were again closed. The lilac air swirled around them. "Kerry was in love with Ms. Peters," he said at last. "That's what she told me. And Ms. Peters loved her too."

"Love. Really?"

"Yes, I think so."

"It's not quite the same, and it's weird. But I'll take some consolation from that." After a moment, she added, "So you're saying Gayle Peters loved Kerry and then . . . and then she pushed her off a cliff?" Her voice trembled.

"I don't think she pushed her off. I don't know what happened," said Ricky.

"Either way, Gayle is so calculating she decides to fabricate a suicide story to save her own skin. What kind of love is that, then?" This wasn't aggressive, just baffled.

Ricky was baffled too. "I don't know as much about Ms. Peters as I do about Kerry. What I do know is that Kerry loved Ms. Peters. I've been trying to remember exactly what she told me. Kerry said she was sad to have to end the relationship. More than sad. Because she talked about how beautiful it was, how she felt so alive and so in love. It was all amazing to me."

"Did she say why she had to end the relationship?" asked Francine.

"She said she had to end it because it was doomed anyway. There was no future in it, she said. And she said, if they continued, people would find out sooner or later."

They both leaned back in their rocking chairs, and Ricky finished off his iced tea.

"But Kerry also told me," he returned to the earlier point, "that she felt Ms. Peters loved her back. I don't know if I believe that myself. I'm sorry—I don't really know what I'm saying, Ms. Loughlin."

"It's helpful, Ricky," said Francine, "you telling me these things."

Ricky rolled on. "I heard that Ms. Peters was charged by the prosecutors with rape. That can't be right. If anyone raped Kerry, it was me."

"No, Ricky."

"Because it was me who violated her sanctity."

She studied Ricky. "No," she scolded. "For one thing, words are not actions. But more important than that, you were speaking what you believed—"

"I was trying to control her," Ricky interrupted.

"It was wrong, Ricky, I grant you that." Francine felt weary. "But don't take on more than you own. You were Kerry's friend, Ricky. You are the one who met with her and talked with her about the most important things going on in her life. When she most needed to confide. It was you, not anyone else. Not her mother."

Ricky heaved a sigh. Francine got up and went into the house, the screen banging, and she returned with a full glass for Ricky.

Ricky thanked her. He gathered himself and spoke again. "May I ask you something else?" She nodded her assent. "Did you know that Kerry and Ms. Peters were having this thing?"

"No, I didn't. No. I knew something was up, Ricky, but not that. Kerry and I did share a lot, but she kept some secrets from me. Obviously. I should have known, right?"

"I don't think so, Ms. Loughlin. Francine. Like, how could she tell you? If you knew, what would you have done?"

"What would I have done," she repeated.

The sound of crunching gravel caught their attention. The police car pulled up the driveway at the side of the house and Barry LaPorte got out and eased up onto the porch. "Well now," he observed.

"She got six years," he said to Francine, kissing the top of her head.

❧

The Jacobsons lingered at the reception following the funeral for Lucy Cross in Jefferson Center. There were baked goods, including lemon squares and something called hazelnut-crunch bars, and conversations. By the time they got on the road, fog had rolled into the valleys and the roads were wet. In decent weather and without mishaps, the trip took over two hours.

There is no straight shot. There is a sequence of route changes, from gravel to paved road back to gravel, through Gunningford and Slade Frey Hill, and other smaller villages, and then busy Route 100 from Stowe, and the last leg on the Interstate to Montpelier.

But not long after leaving the reception, on the stretch between Slade Frey Hill and South Slade Frey, they were delayed as a farmer led his herd, aching to be milked, from pasture on the west side of the road to their barn across the road on the east. Freed from the cattle crossing, they were then stuck behind a slow-moving tractor that obliviously took up the full lane before an opportunity to pass came a mile or two later.

Donna was asleep by then, and Sam was grumbling to himself with All Things Considered at low volume on the radio. The Republicans had fielded a score of candidates vying for the party's nomination for the presidency, and the very least qualified one was pulling ahead of his rivals by boasting of his singular greatness and mocking his adversaries with schoolyard taunts. This is what passes for politics now, Sam thought. His only comfort was the thought that this nadir would surely pass.

Donna woke up when they came to Jeffordsville, where they stopped for a bathroom break. Back in the car, she told him tales from her work: the Deputy Commissioner had been fired after pornography was discovered on his computer; one of Donna's clients had sued the agency alleging religious discrimination when it declined to reimburse the client for travel costs to attend AA meetings.

Taking Route 100 turned out to be a mistake too, as traffic jammed the highway around Stowe where a thousand eager tourists milled about for the annual antique automobile festival. And in Waterbury Center, early-season tour buses leaving the Ben & Jerry's factory locked up traffic once more. It was a long trip home, and Sam Jacobson was cranky. At least the weather was better in Montpelier.

Sarah had already welcomed the three Stillwells to the house. They were outside on the side deck, the sun slanting across with a warm glow on the crabapple trees, and Sarah was plying them with iced tea and chips and salsa and cheese and crackers when Sam and Donna wheeled in the drive. For a minute, Sam watched them from inside the car.

They seemed at ease. He couldn't hear, but could see their expressions and talk and laughter. Wary Ricky, silent Carver, bitter Clara—none of that was evident. "You coming up, old man?" said Donna, holding the car door for him.

"Look at that," he said. "The four of them look like they're having a good time."

"And you're surprised because?"

"Because I'm a miserable misanthrope. I don't expect people to get along. At least not the Stillwell parents with Sarah. Ricky, I'll admit, has grown out of his worst delusions."

"That's true," she said.

"And you've invited Barb and Alicia," he went on. "What were you thinking? I can't imagine Clara Stillwell is even going to look at Alicia. Let alone share stories. They are from different centuries. Different species."

"You are wrong about that," Donna said. "You'll see."

Behind them, Barb and Alicia pulled up the driveway in their Passat. "Okay to park here?" called Alicia, not waiting for an answer. She got out, hefting an enormous pyrex bowl covered in foil. "Pasta with pesto," she explained. "Mmmm. Smell the fresh pesto?" She looked in at Sam with her beautiful therapeutic grin, and he got himself out of his car, kissing first Alicia and then Barb, who also bore a baby spinach salad, enough to feed twelve.

On the deck, Clara exchanged gracious greetings with Alicia and Barb, and Carver bobbed his head in cordial acknowledgment. Sarah had fetched a bottle of merlot and wine glasses from the kitchen. Donna poured for herself and the other arrivals. Sarah and Ricky retreated to the kitchen.

Donna advanced on the cheese board, cut a chunk of Spanish manchego, sliced off the black rippled wax, deliciously oily in her fingers, and pressed the cheese between a couple of table wafers. "Here you go, Sam. Manchego. You deserve it," and she delicately placed it in his mouth.

"I don't deserve anything," he mumbled through the cracker. "This is wonderful." He swirled merlot in his mouth following the cheese.

"Wonderful cheese, wonderful camaraderie," said Donna. "You do see it now," the motion of her head encompassing the opinionated characters gathered in social communion on their deck.

"Smug, are we?" he posited.

As the golden sun fell below the horizon and the temperature dropped into the fifties, the party moved inside. Carver had baked a loaf of oat bread, and Clara had made lentil stew. Sam put some asparagus spears to steam in a pan on the stove. Alicia and Barb were proselytizing to Carver on the virtues of yoga, encouraging him to join their Saturday morning workouts at the Downward Dog. He had no clue.

"It's in the space above Colten's Hardware," Alicia explained. "People wear spandex," she explained further, with glee.

"Don't have any," said Carver.

Clara stood at the stove, next to Sam, as she warmed the lentil stew over a gas flame. "Sam," she offered, "I never properly thanked you for helping Ricky and us in the legal case. It made a big difference."

"That's no problem, Clara. He's such a good kid. Even though, well, I didn't agree with those things he wrote about homosexuality. It seems he has modified his views for the better, don't you think? Perhaps you don't agree?" He was stumbling, unsure.

"Sam, you *know* I don't agree," she said, but with warm solicitude.

Sam righted himself. "Did you hear Ricky came to watch me argue a case in New York? I was tremendously glad to see him. He seems to be doing really well at NYU."

"Yes, he is. He's growing up so much. I have to admit he's happier. To tell the truth, Sam, I'm pleased he left that Fellowship Church. Carver and I were never fans of that church." Sam's surprise showed on his face. "What, you thought we *liked* that church? No!"

"I didn't know that, Clara. I'm sorry. I should pay more attention to certain things. I guess I focus too much on my own world."

"Don't we all. About your legal case in New York, Ricky did tell me he went to see that. That was an honor for him, you know. It was the case about the prayer at town meeting? Ricky agrees with your position. I'm not sure I do, but that's all right. I just feel so often that our culture has become hostile to religion, and that's a shame. Let's leave that aside for now."

Donna, overhearing bits of the conversation as she stood by the counter mixing oil and vinegar for the salad, found herself watching Ricky. He was moving around Sarah at the other end of the kitchen, where a table fit closely into an alcove, as if he were dancing, this lanky awkward boy sliding gracefully around Sarah, brushing her shoulder as he passed, and Sarah glanced up at him with the play of a smile on her lips.

Clara noticed too. "Do you see what I see?" she said, reminding Donna of the Christmas carol. "With such a difference in their ages!"

"What are we talking about?" Sam asked.

"Well, counselor," Clara said, "keep your eye on your daughter."

"What?" he asked again.

"Look at those two, Sam." Donna nodded her head toward the alcove where Ricky and Sarah, standing closer than needed, were putting out place settings. Sam did so, and at the same moment Sarah looked up from her task, caught her father's gaze, and turned red. Then slowly she smiled.

"It's providence," declared Clara. "These two were meant to be."

"Oh, for God's sake," Sam sputtered.

"Hush up," said Donna.

"Dammit," said Sam in confusion, "you made me overcook the asparagus. They've gone all limp." He held one up with a fork for Donna to see.

"Everything changes shape now," he said. "Nothing is simple anymore."

Acknowledgments

A number of true friends were put upon to read early drafts of this novel and to offer critical feedback: John Page, Margery Colten, Dorothy Tegeler, Jeannie Elias, Cindy Hier, Tanya Broder, Sara Campos, Tom Vitzthum, and Lynn Cleveland Vitzthum. I am so grateful to them. My father, Joachim Lambek, encouraged me at an early stage too, though he told me "out" cannot be used as a verb. I am sorry the final version came too late for him.

I owe profound thanks to the marvelous novelist Howard Norman, who generously nurtured me as a fiction writer and told me quite early on, "You have a real novel here," an affirmation that sparked me to pursue the writing.

Jim Morse, the retired Vermont Supreme Court Justice for whom I clerked at the beginning of my legal career, found some legal loopholes I had neglected to close. The Vermont raconteur and essayist Bill Schubart gave me valuable critical advice. Yale Law Professor Stephen Wizner and the eminent British novelist Simon Mawer, whose novel *The Glass Room* is a fictional account of my grandmother Grete Tugendhat's house in Brno, both kindly read the almost-final manuscript. Second Circuit Court of Appeals Judge Guido Calabresi, Dean at the Yale Law School when I was a student there, graciously allowed me to appropriate him as a character in this novel and to put fictional words in his mouth. I am deeply indebted to all of them.

I cannot thank enough my wise publisher Stephen McArthur at Rootstock Publishing and my brilliant editor Rickey Gard Diamond, who have worked with me on this book with unfailing support, guidance and expertise. And my old friend Susan Bull Riley, a painter of astonishing talent, who allowed *Winter Morning, Elm Street* to appear on the cover of this book.

For showing me how one best pursues a moral, just and gleeful life, I thank my sons, Dom, Matt and Will. Finally I am immensely grateful to my loving and tolerant wife, Linda Sproul.

About The Author

Bernie Lambek grew up in Montreal, the son of Jewish refugees from Nazi Europe. He studied philosophy at Dartmouth College, lived on a communal farm, and taught fourth grade for several years. He later attended Yale Law School, where he published articles on civil disobedience and international human rights. After judicial clerkships, including with Judge Fred Parker on the Second Circuit Court of Appeals, Lambek has practiced law at Zalinger Cameron & Lambek in Montpelier, Vermont, for the past 25 years. He represents a number of school districts around Vermont, occasionally dealing with issues of student speech and religion in the schools. In a 2012 lawsuit, Lambek and ACLU colleagues successfully challenged the practice of holding official prayer at town meeting in Vermont. Lambek serves on the Boards of the Vermont ACLU and the Green Mountain Film Festival. His wife, Linda Sproul, is a retired obstetric and pediatric nurse and they have three sons and four grandchildren. He plays table tennis and recently competed in the National Senior Games in Birmingham, AL. *Uncivil Liberties* is his first novel.

CPSIA information can be obtained
at www.ICGtesting.com
Printed in the USA
BVHW04s2204280518
517604BV00001B/99/P